Coconut Dreams

Coconut Dreams

stories by
Derek Mascarenhas

BOOK*HUG PRESS 2019

FIRST EDITION

The production of this book was made possible through the generous assistance of the Canada Council for the Arts and the Ontario Arts Council. Book*hug Press also acknowledges the support of the Government of Canada through the Canada Book Fund and the Government of Ontario through the Ontario Book Publishing Tax Credit and the Ontario Book Fund.

Book*hug Press acknowledges the land on which it operates. For thousands of years it has been the traditional land of the Huron-Wendat, the Seneca, and most recently, the Mississaugas of the Credit River. Today, this meeting place is still the home to many Indigenous people from across Turtle Island, and we are grateful to have the opportunity to work on this land.

LIBRARY AND ARCHIVES CANADA CATALOGUING IN PUBLICATION

Title: Coconut dreams / stories by Derek Mascarenhas.
Names: Mascarenhas, Derek, [date]—author.
Description: Short stories.
Identifiers: Canadiana (print) 20190076720 | Canadiana (ebook) 20190076739

ISBN 9781771664813 (softcover)
ISBN 9781771664820 (HTML)
ISBN 9781771664837 (PDF)
ISBN 9781771664844 (Kindle)

Classification: LCC PS8626.A795 C64 2019 | DDC C813/.6—dc23

PRINTED IN CANADA

For my family.

Contents

The Call of the Bell

May 25, 1946

Felix Pinto's birth in a cemetery was never forgotten by the village of Colvale. Mysteries, like tragedies, are long remembered.

Felix's mother, Rosetta, attended the funeral of her former elementary school teacher that morning. While she was trying, and failing, to squeeze her pregnant belly into her best black outfits, Felix's father, Miguel, wearing dark slacks and a dress shirt, suggested she stay home and rest. "Even the monkeys stop running on the roofs in this heat."

"I'm not a monkey, and I don't intend to run on any roof." Rosetta finally pulled a brown dress down over her belly; fifteen days overdue, she was rounder than she'd ever been with her two previous pregnancies.

"You should stay and rest."

"Miguel, I've known Mr. Lopez since I was a girl. The least I can do is attend the service."

The house was quiet. Rosetta and Miguel's two sons had already returned to Bombay to get ready for school. The boys'

Nunna had accompanied them, so Rosetta wouldn't have to make such a long journey so close to the baby's arrival.

"At least let us try to catch a ride at the road, then."

Rosetta nodded. It wasn't far to the church, but she knew Miguel wanted to feel useful. He fixed machines in the cotton mills. He needed to fix things, but not all of life's problems could be solved with the same mechanical exactitude.

On their way to the main road they saw a bullock cart approaching. The cartload of coconuts was pulled by two giant oxen with coats, eyes, and wet noses the same jet-black colour; their white horns curved skyward.

Miguel waved the driver down.

"I'm heading to the Mapusa market, but I can drop you at the church on the way," the driver said, and gestured to the back. "As long as your husband is okay sitting on the coconuts, Madam, you can join me up front."

As the driver helped Rosetta into the passenger seat, she noticed the sinewy muscles in his forearms, concluding that he must also climb the coconut trees himself.

With Rosetta up front and Miguel settled atop the many green, football-sized fruits, the driver gave the oxen a tap on their rears with a thin bamboo stick; the cart rolled through the humid air, the oxen's heads bobbing and dust billowing behind them.

The cemetery was adjacent to the tall stone church built by the Portuguese. The church, painted a bright seashell-white, stood in sharp contrast to the jade palms and indigo river behind it, and the ground of tiny, red xencare. These small stones had been rounded by rain on their journey down from the high hills.

Rosetta and Miguel thanked the driver as he got back on his cart. Miguel asked him if he was taking the hill path to

Mapusa, pointing to a dirt trail that started at the cemetery and led straight up the hill to a lone, empty house at the top. Rosetta's brother claimed that the house was haunted, though most houses that stayed empty for long were conferred that status.

"It's the fastest route. I need to let the oxen drink by the river first, though." The driver gave another tap on the oxen's rear, but one of the animals groaned and bucked, nudging a single coconut off the cart. It hit the ground with a thud. Miguel picked it up and handed it back to the driver, who smiled, embarrassed, at the animal's disobedience.

"Good luck at the market," Rosetta said, as they waved goodbye.

Miguel led Rosetta by the hand to the crowd gathering outside the church. "So many people," he said.

"He was well-liked."

Mr. Lopez's quiet kindness had been his way of conveying an innate belief in every student's potential. It was what brought most of his graduates back to visit him years later. Rosetta had gone back to ask Mr. Lopez's advice many times herself.

The bell tower chimed every few seconds to let everyone know the service was starting. Shielding her eyes from the sun, Rosetta could see the silhouette of the bell operator up in the tower swinging the bell's rope. She had heard his signal the night before: the prolonged gap he'd left between each of the three chimes had indicated that someone from the village had died.

The crowd parted to let Rosetta through. She gave them a funeral-appropriate half-smile. In spite of this, her dimples still showed. Everyone's eyes were on her belly, a bulging jackfruit ready to drop.

Miguel helped Rosetta to a seat near the back of the church after a few parishioners made room. She was thankful to sit once again; a short distance felt like a marathon in the day's sweltering heat.

Once everyone was sitting, Father Constantine stepped up to the pulpit. His bushy grey eyebrows rested above thick rectangular glasses, and he rushed through the mass as if it were community announcements.

As he spoke, Rosetta eyed the closed coffin of simple, unvarnished wood at the front of the church. She had heard that the only thing included with the body of their beloved schoolteacher was his iron walking stick, and pictured it now, folded in his hands.

After the mass concluded, Father Constantine led a procession of pallbearers outside. Rosetta let the rest of the congregation exit first, before she followed with Miguel. She felt the blazing sun as soon as she got outside and took her time walking past the stone statue of St. Francis of Assisi—painted the same seashell-white as the church—to the shade offered by the cemetery walls and trees. Mr. Lopez had once told Rosetta and the rest of her class—to prevent them from cutting through the cemetery—that those walls weren't built to keep people out but to keep spirits in.

Rosetta's friend Nina intercepted her halfway.

"Have you seen Noah?" she whispered, sweat on her forehead and worry in her eyes. "He normally works late, and if he doesn't come home he stays at his brother's, so I wasn't worried. But I just saw his brother in the church and he said Noah didn't come over last night."

"Maybe he's still at his office?" Miguel suggested.

"I hope so. I'll go check as soon as the service is over."

Miguel, Rosetta, and Nina joined the crowd gathered around the grave. The muggy air was heavy, absent the mercy of even the faintest breeze. Rosetta could feel the sweat under her arms and breasts. She shifted her weight in discomfort but couldn't get comfortable; Miguel stepped behind her, letting her lean back into him.

As Father Constantine flicked the coffin with holy water from a silver aspergillum, he mumbled Latin prayers that Rosetta and most of the village didn't understand. Before the coffin was lowered into the ground, he called for a final moment of silence. During this time at funerals, the silence was often broken by a murmur, sniffle, or sob. Occasionally, mourners were so overcome with emotion that they wailed and cried; rarely, someone would actually faint. But today, when the quiet was interrupted, it was not by one of the mourners.

A cry for help came from above.

The voice seemed to emanate from the top of a tall palm tree beside the cemetery. And within its fronds, Rosetta saw a waving arm.

The voice shouted, "Nina!"

Nina raised a hand to her forehead to block the sun. "Noah? How did you get up there?"

"I don't know. Help me get down."

A woman from the crowd hollered, "Why don't you climb down?"

"I don't know how. I need help."

"Fetch Diego," someone else suggested, "he'll handle this."

Rosetta felt the baby move, followed by Miguel giving her hand a squeeze and then releasing it. "I'll go run and get the boys by the river," he offered.

Rosetta thought maybe it was a mistake to let him go, but he returned with three boys and a coiled rope, which one of the boys put around his waist before they climbed up the tree, one then the next in tandem. The boys hugged the tree and curved their feet around the trunk, shimmying up half body lengths at a time. Once up top, they tied the rope around Noah's waist and began to lower him to the ground as if he were a cluster of tender coconuts.

Rosetta watched from below. The boys had the same sinewy strength in their limbs that she had noticed in the bullock-cart driver. Noah's body, dangling like a tea bag on a string, was comparatively short and pudgy, and his limbs flailed like those of a caught insect.

Nina ran over and hugged Noah. Disoriented, he asked for water. A clay jug was fetched from the church, and as Noah drank and regained his composure, Diego rode up on his white horse. He had broad shoulders, a thin moustache, and wore the khaki-coloured uniform of the Portuguese officials, complete with black leather boots, navy blue blazer, and matching hat, brimmed on only the left side.

Diego nodded to Father Constantine, who stood impatiently beside the grave, Bible in hand.

From atop his horse, Diego addressed Noah. "So I hear you got stuck in a tree. How did that happen?"

"I don't know. Last I remember I was on my way home."

"But how does that get you up a tree?"

"Arrey, I told you, I don't know." He shook his head from side to side. "I woke up, and I was up there."

The crowd murmured nervously. Nina made the sign of the cross, and the act spread to others around her.

Diego turned to Father Constantine. "We can discuss this later. For now, Father, please continue the service."

Father Constantine made a show of clearing his throat, and took his time opening the Bible to the exact place he'd left off.

As the last of the flowers were placed on top of the grave, Rosetta felt an overwhelming wave of heat and exhaustion. With tears flowing down her cheeks, she felt it: a sudden warmth.

Miguel mistook Rosetta's tears for mourning and handed her

his handkerchief, which Rosetta twisted in her hands. Water began running down her legs as the crowd filtered out of the cemetery. They were anxious to get out of the sun and properly gossip about how Noah had really ended up in that tree—a prank, or maybe even a malicious spirit.

Miguel put an arm around Rosetta but pulled away upon noticing the wet spot on her brown dress.

Rosetta felt a pain much sharper than she had in her previous pregnancies, and dropped to the ground. Miguel called her name, gripping her shoulders in panic. He helped her lean against the gravestone beside Mr. Lopez's grave, then ran for help, shouting to the crowd now outside the cemetery walls.

Through the cemetery entrance, Rosetta watched as Miguel was intercepted by a hard and heavy green coconut rolling down the hill to Mapusa, tripping him and sending him to the ground. Rosetta cried after him, and for a moment he lay there. Then a low rumbling noise followed. A landslide of coconuts was coming down the hill toward the crowd.

As the first coconuts began rolling underfoot, Diego's horse rose up on its hind legs and kicked its two front legs in the air, throwing him to the ground. A wave of coconuts followed and knocked people over; those who kept their feet collided in the scramble to dodge the tropical avalanche.

When it was over, and the final coconut had gone bouncing off into the churchyard, everyone had been felled except Rosetta, protected by the cemetery wall. She watched as some people got to their feet. Others remained on the ground, moaning and clutching their legs where the coconuts had struck.

The bullock-cart driver came running down the hill, out of breath. He put both hands on his head when he saw the scene outside the cemetery.

"What happened? Are these your coconuts?" Diego asked him.

"Yes, but it wasn't my fault. I was on my way to Mapusa, but when I approached the house at the top"—he pointed up to the hill, still trying to catch his breath—"I saw a pineapple fall down from the zamblam tree out front."

"Pineapples don't grow on trees," Diego said.

"That's why I stopped. But the oxen startled. The cart tipped backwards. And all my coconuts were sent rolling down the hill. I was lucky I wasn't crushed!"

Rosetta felt a sharp pain and cried out. A few yards away, Miguel had regained his sense. "Rosetta is in labour," he cried. "We have to help her!"

He arrived with a few villagers to discover Rosetta panting, blood flowing between her legs. "We need to go to the hospital," Miguel said, but Rosetta shook her head. No time. The baby was coming.

An older woman who used to be a midwife was hurried over. She ordered others nearby to run and fetch hot water, a clean cloth and a knife, and a tincture from the Ayurvedic doctor for the pain.

The next moments were a blur for Rosetta: calm voices trying to coach her, waves of pain, panic, fluids, and contractions; it felt as if the life itself were flowing out from her.

The xencare on the ground were stained a darker red as Felix Pinto let out his first cry: piercing, high-pitched, and unnatural amongst the graves.

Normally, the birth of a child in Goa brought sweets and celebrations. Firecrackers would be lit shortly after the birth to announce the occasion: three firecrackers for a boy and two for a girl. Instead, at his wife's bedside in the hospital, still holding her limp and lifeless hand, Miguel listened to the slow ringing of the church bell, the long spaces between each toll signalling another death.

Time passed, and the village of Colvale's feelings about that day gradually shifted from grief to superstition. Rumours spread of a new noise in the night at the top of the hill to Mapusa: a rare metal twang, like an iron rod reverberating off stone. Some said Mr. Lopez had been too busy watching the events of that day and missed his chance to ascend to heaven. Legend also grew about the house at the top of the hill. How it had sat empty for many years. How, because the owners had cheated the labourers who had built it, when they died, their souls were forced to stay in the house instead of moving on to the next world.

A detour in the path to Mapusa was built through the trees to skirt the house, but other things were not so easily avoided.

May 17, 1958

The church bell chimed for the evening angelus, and Clara said to Felix Pinto, "Time to go."

The two friends sat beneath a zamblam tree on the edge of the forest. Although the tree was an infant compared to the centurion it would one day become, berry-like fruit filled its branches and scattered on the ground below.

"Are you getting scared?" Felix tossed one last sweet and mildly sour zamblam into his mouth. His hands and teeth were stained by the juicy purple flesh.

"No," said Clara. But she marked her page in her Enid Blyton book and stood.

"It's just a silly saying," Felix said. The rhyme used to scare children popped into his head: *In the afternoon between twelve and three, the ghosts come out under the zamblam tree.*

"I know," Clara said.

Felix wasn't fully convinced; Clara was two years younger than him and more likely to believe in ghosts, but he said, "Chalo. Let's go, then." He got up and returned his slingshot to his front pocket. He pointed to the road where a bullock cart, stacked high with hay, rolled along. "There's our ride home!"

Sneaking up behind the cart so the driver couldn't see them over his high load of hay, Felix first lifted himself up, then helped Clara.

They leaned back against the hay, watching the rolling hill-side planted with cashew trees; the cash crop carpeted the hills green.

"I can't wait for the cashews this week," said Clara. The actual feast of St. Francis of Assisi was in September, but the village celebration took place in May to avoid the monsoon and take advantage of the children being on summer holidays.

"And the kadio bodio." Felix was just imagining the sugary pretzel stick covered in nuts when he remembered the anniversary of his mother's death always fell a few days after the celebration; this year also marked his twelfth birthday.

He then saw riders on horseback gaining on the cart from the rear, led by Diego on his white horse. A small spotted deer, freshly killed, was draped over the horse's neck.

"Quick, hide!" said Felix. They both tried to bury themselves in the hay.

The riders passed on the right. Felix poked out his head to see if they were gone, but Diego was turning back to stop the driver, so he and Clara dove back under the hay as the cart pulled off the road outside Tinto's, a tea stall famous for its homemade liquors.

"Come out of there!"

At Diego's command, Felix and Clara jumped down from the cart without arguing and brushed the hay from their clothes. Diego waved his arm at the driver, and as the bullock cart resumed its journey, he whistled to his friends, telling them he'd catch up. Then he turned back to the stowaways, towering over them on his horse.

"You two are old enough to know not to sneak on the back of a cart like that. You could get hurt if it tips over."

Felix cast his eyes to the dusty red earth.

Diego softened, and pointed to Felix's slingshot. "Have you been practising your shot?"

"Every day," Felix replied.

Clara, eyeing the creature around the horse's neck, asked, "Did you kill that cheetal in the forest?"

"Yes, but you two please don't get any ideas. The forest is much more dangerous than a bullock cart, especially at night."

At this point, Wagh Marea emerged from Tinto's, staggering over with a bottle of cashew fenny. "I see you've caught a small animal, Diego," he said, more confident with his words than with his gait.

"Yes, but—"

"I once killed a full-grown tiger on a hunt." Wagh puffed his thin chest out like a proud child and took a swig from the bottle.

Diego shook his head. "You shouldn't drink that in front of children."

Wagh briefly eyed Felix and Clara, as if just noticing them. Felix's father had used fenny to start a fire, and when his older brother Jacob snuck a swig, he coughed for two minutes.

"But how many men have tugged a tiger by the tail and lived to tell of it?" demanded Wagh.

Diego raised his voice. "We hadn't set out on a hunt."

"Ah, so the hunt found you."

"There have been sightings of strange men in the forest coming from Chikhli. That's what we went to investigate." Diego turned back to Felix and Clara. "Another reason for you not to go there. Now, I suggest you two get going home." Diego tipped his hat to Wagh, spurred his horse, and rode off.

Wagh's body deflated. But then he tensed and shouted, "Lousy packlo! Thinks he's so much better than us."

"We'd like to hear your tiger story next time," Felix said, as they turned to go.

"Us outcasts have to stick together," Wagh shouted back with a raised bottle, and Felix and Clara hurried home on foot.

The last of the day's light was fading as Felix parted ways with Clara at her home, a squat yellow building that sat behind a weathered stone wall and two papaya trees.

Felix continued the short distance to his own home, picking up his pace as he passed Mrs. Rocha's. From her porch, the old woman shot an unwelcoming stare at him, as if he were a black cat crossing her path. Mrs. Rocha did have the most beautiful bougainvilleas; the white and pink blooms covered the stone wall around her house. Felix often wondered how such a rotten person could sit behind such a pretty sight.

He hurried along to his house, opened the low metal gate, and ran up the verandah to discover his Nunna ironing dress shirts for church the next morning.

"So late you've come," she remarked.

"Are Nicholas and Jacob home?"

"Your brothers are older, Felix. And they came home to bathe and eat already." Felix's Nunna dipped her hand into a bowl of water and flicked droplets onto the shirt's front. The small iron had hot coals inside, and when she ran it across the shirt, steam rose to the ceiling.

She finished the last shirt with a few deft presses and hung it on a hanger. She then walked over to Felix, her bad knee causing a slight limp, and gave him a kiss on the forehead with her wrinkled lips. "Go eat. I kept your food out." Then she added: "And go quietly past your father. He might still be asleep."

Felix was blessed with his mother's dimpled smile and he

shared it with his Nunna. He had learned not to smile this way to his father; it triggered a slow and sad remembrance in him.

The hard cow-dung floor was cool against Felix's bare feet. He tiptoed past the bedroom but jumped when he heard his father's voice.

"Felix. Come here."

Miguel was sitting on the bed, feet on the ground and shirtless. The room smelled of cigarettes.

"Where have you been?"

"Just out playing with Clara."

"Let me see your hands."

Felix held out his hands, eyeing the thin bamboo cane standing in the corner.

When Miguel saw the purple stains, he shouted, "You know what they say about those trees!"

"But it wasn't afternoon."

"Do you want the schoolteacher haunting us?" Miguel made a move toward the cane but stopped himself. "And involving Clara. You're going to lose your only friend. Now go wash your hands of that evil."

The twilit sky reflected in the water at the bottom of the backyard well, shattered by the pail as it crashed below. Washing his hands, Felix thought about how his Nunna had told him that it was only after his mother had died that his father had become superstitious. She'd told Felix this to make him feel better, but it had the opposite effect—and everything became even worse when the anniversary of his mother's death approached each year.

Only the week before, Miguel had erupted when they were collecting mangoes. Felix had been using his slingshot to knock the fruit from their backyard tree. His aim was excellent—he fired stones through the tree's foliage and hit only the stems, so the ripe mangoes dropped down to his brothers below. Jacob and Nicholas jostled one another to catch the falling fruit. "Great job, Felix," Nicholas said. With their father watching from the kitchen window, Felix felt proud and useful. But then Jacob smirked and said, "Yeah, almost makes up for killing our mom." Enraged, Felix took aim at Jacob with the slingshot, holding it taut. He wanted to hurt his eldest brother, but something made him miss, and the stone landed in a hole in the yard, beside the stone fence.

Miguel rushed outside. "There's a snake living in that hole! Are you trying to bring more curses on this family? It will remember our scents and come to take revenge at night. Now go see the Shinari."

Obediently Felix went to the holy man, who gave him rice blessed with prayers. The Shinari wouldn't take money, for fear of losing his God-given powers, so in exchange Felix had to give him the mangoes he'd collected, along with a week's worth of bananas, and when he returned home, Miguel made Felix spread the rice around the entire perimeter of their house so the snake wouldn't enter.

The sun was down by the time Felix washed most of the purple from his hands. He remembered his dad's warning about the schoolteacher, and before going back inside, he paused and stared at the almost full moon, thankful that at least his mother hadn't also been turned into a ghost that haunted the village.

Felix sat with his family at Sunday-morning mass, and Clara with hers, but they caught each other's eye when Father Constantine fell asleep after Communion. Felix tilted his head on his flattened palm to mimic a pillow, and Clara nodded. The priest was old, and it was sometimes difficult to tell if his eyes were open or not, but as the hymn ended it became clear he was asleep. The altar servers had already put the gold chalices away and returned to their seats. The rest of the congregation knelt in their pews, waiting for Father to stand, but he remained sitting.

Felix motioned to Clara to look at a few of the younger children, who had also sensed what was happening. The kids swivelled around looking for confirmation, their eyes full of delight. The adults managed to keep the children in line before their laughter spread.

Eventually, the organist started a new hymn, skilfully emphasizing some of the deeper notes. When he saw Father rousing, he quickly concluded the piece. Unaware of any aberration, Father rose, and the rest of the congregation followed.

After mass, Felix and Clara walked home together to change out of their church clothes, then reunited under the bright yellow flowers of the golden rain tree—Clara's choice.

"Are you hunting bats with your brothers tonight?" Clara asked.

"It's a full moon, isn't it?"

"I don't know why you go with them. They're so mean to you."

"You wouldn't understand." Felix looked past her, eyeing a carriage coming down the road. It was small, but fancier than most he had seen.

"Why, because I'm a girl? They only invite you because you're the best shot," Clara said, but Felix ignored her: the horse pulling the carriage was as white as Diego's, and the driver wore all black. This was odd, as few people wore black in the heat of summer, unless they were in mourning. But then, as the carriage slowed to a stop next to them, Felix noticed the driver's white collar.

"Hello, could either of you direct me to the church?" The priest had neatly parted, coffee-coloured hair, his skin as smooth as a boy's and lighter than that of the native Goans in the village.

Felix stepped forward, pointing. "Just down the road and to the left."

"Much appreciated." The priest bowed his head slightly. "My name is Salvador Barroso, your new priest."

Both Felix's and Clara's eyes lit up, unaware they were getting a new priest and excited to be the first in the village to meet him.

"Where did you come from?" Felix asked.

"All the way from Lisbon, my young man."

"You met him?" Jacob asked Felix. Felix sat with his older brothers near the edge of the forest around a small fire they'd made from dry palm leaves and sticks. Nicholas held a stick over the fire with one of the flying fox bats impaled on it. The bat's hair was singed off and the smell of roasted meat hung in the air.

"Yeah, I talked to him for a while and told him where the church was," Felix said. He was surprised how fast news had spread through the village. People who normally wouldn't talk to him had asked about the new priest. Felix's father even said they'd all meet him tomorrow on the feast day; usually when his family talked to Father Constantine after mass, he was excluded.

"I heard Father Constantine didn't even know the bishop was sending anyone." Nicholas removed the bat from the fire and broke off a piece of steaming meat before he passed it around. The flying foxes gorged on fruit and nectar, so their flesh was more tender and tasty than any chicken or pork.

The boys had snuck out of their home with flashlights to visit the guava and chikoo trees where the bats fed. The full moon made it easier to locate the bats high up in the trees, and then they used the flashlights to stun them. Although all three brothers fired rocks with their slingshots, only Felix's shot hit: tonight he'd killed both bats.

"He's so old, he probably just forgot," Jacob said, a piece of the cooked meat in his mouth. The way Jacob talked while eating annoyed Felix, the food smacking noisily around. Then he proceeded to lick his fingers.

Nicholas said, "Do you remember the story of how Father Constantine tried to exorcise that haunted house at the top of the hill?"

"Yeah, the door slammed shut when he started saying prayers, and his cap disappeared," said Jacob, inserting another piece of meat in his mouth, "so he ran from the house with his Bible in his hand."

His brothers' laughter bothered Felix. "Every year that story gets more exaggerated. When I first heard it, there was no door slamming or cap disappearing."

"Our brother doesn't believe in ghosts," Jacob said to Nicholas, "despite being born among them."

Felix was reminded of what Clara had said about his brothers. Maybe she was right. He speared the second bat through its mouth with a stick and held it over the flame. The fire crackled, then sizzled as fat dripped down into it.

"If you really don't believe in ghosts, then go into that house." Jacob stared at Felix. "I bet you won't."

The moon lit the way as the brothers walked past the cemetery where their mother was buried and past the statue of St. Francis of Assisi, up the hill to the haunted house.

"What's that noise?" Jacob asked.

"What noise?" Nicholas said.

"You don't hear that banging?"

Felix couldn't hear anything, but judging by the smirk on

Jacob's face, he knew what his brother was going to say next.

"Must be the schoolteacher. You know what they say—he roams these paths. If you keep walking, he'll protect you, but if you look back, he'll get you for sure."

"Felix, you better hope he protects you," Nicholas added.

Felix, silent, kept walking up the hill, but as they approached the top and he saw the property overrun by vegetation, his toes tingled with each step.

The boys passed under the giant zamblam tree in the front yard, their feet crunching through stray palm fronds, greedy shrubs, and dead leaves that hid the red-stoned earth, and stopped in front of the house. The roof and walls were covered in vines that had been dried by the summer heat and were waiting for the monsoon to grow green again.

"Well?" Nicholas finally said.

Felix marched up to the house to show he was not afraid, though he swallowed as he neared the door, hoping it was locked. No luck: the door was slightly ajar, with a crack leading to darkness. As he pulled it open, the door scraped on the dirt ground. Moonlight illuminated the entrance, but no further, and Felix swept his flashlight ahead of him as he entered.

The main room, other than a small table and rocking chair, was empty of furniture, and the air was stale. Felix took slow steps to the rocking chair. He could hear his brothers talking outside. As he was peering down the hallway, the front door slammed shut behind him. The moonlight vanished and Felix was left with the single beam of his flashlight. The seclusion sent a fright through him, and he shone the light erratically at different spots in the room, expecting to find the schoolteacher rising out of the dark.

Laughter filtered in from outside. Felix went to the door and tried pushing it open, but something was blocking it. "Nicholas! Let me out!" Felix banged on the door. "Jacob!"

No response.

When he got out, he would fire so many stones at them, and never again miss on purpose. Felix slammed his shoulder into the door once more. When it didn't budge, he turned and, following the beam of his flashlight, began to inch down the narrow hallway toward the back of the house, brushing away spiderwebs and passing dark doorways he didn't dare point his flashlight into.

The hallway opened to a backroom. The windows were shuttered yet permitted slices of moonlight into the room. The back door was locked and one of the window shutters was jammed, but Felix was able to open the other window with some effort. Peering outside, he was glad to see the ground a few feet below. He turned off his flashlight and climbed out.

In the backyard was an outhouse covered in the same vines that thickened into the forest. As Felix began creeping around the house, he noticed a light in the forest. It looked like a bonfire with two dark shadows standing in front of it: one broad and looming, the other skinny and sticklike.

A loud *twang* of metal hitting stone rang out. Felix cowered and looked all around. The figures had vanished. Another *twang* reverberated and the bonfire disappeared, too.

When the sound came a third time, he ran.

Heading into the front yard, he tripped in the weeds and dropped his flashlight, which went out as it hit the ground. He didn't pick it up, just kept running, the sound ringing out behind him.

Felix's brothers were gone, but the sound had him scrambling down the hill. He slid and braced himself, and somehow managed not to tumble over on the way down. At the bottom he diverted his eyes from the statue and church and graves, sprinting past. It wasn't until, doubled over and breathing hard, he stopped at Mrs. Rocha's bougainvillea that he realized he couldn't hear the sound anymore.

A hand grabbed his arm.

"Stupid child!" Felix's father yelled. He was wearing a white cotton undershirt and shorts. "What were you thinking going to that house?"

"I—"

"I've already caught your brothers. Don't you lie to me!" Miguel pulled Felix away by the arm. "I told you not to go messing with ghosts."

"There are no such things as ghosts!" Felix blurted out, then cowered, expecting to be hit.

"I'll teach you," his father growled, dragging Felix through the front door of the house and slamming it behind him.

The next morning at mass there wasn't an empty seat in the church. The feast celebration usually attracted more parishioners than the normal weekly service, but the whole village had shown up to meet the new priest.

Felix sat in the back row with his brothers, Nunna, and father. The boys squirmed uncomfortably in their seats, their bottoms raw and swollen. Miguel had given Nicholas and Jacob two whacks each with the cane, but Felix got five for talking back. He could still hear the whir of the cane cutting through the air. In the morning, Felix's Nunna had given them all fresh gel from the aloe plant for their sores, and both Nicholas and Jacob apologized to Felix, looking genuinely sorry. "We were going to let you out but then heard the schoolteacher's noise for real and couldn't go back," Nicholas said. "Did you hear it, too?" Jacob asked.

Felix refused to speak to them. He didn't want to admit he'd heard the same thing. He didn't want to tell them what he'd seen either, as he wasn't sure himself—the fire, the figures. And how they'd just vanished.

The thought that he might indeed be cursed entered Felix's mind as Father Constantine introduced Father Salvador. The shorter members of the congregation and those in the back stood on their tiptoes to catch a better glimpse of the new priest stepping up to the pulpit. Having already met him, Felix let his Nunna have the better view, but she sat back down soon after, rubbing her knee.

Father Salvador thanked Father Constantine and turned to address the congregation. "I'm already overwhelmed by all of the pious people I've met and look forward to becoming part of this community. I'm also thrilled to be able to assist Father Constantine and learn from such a fine and long-standing servant of our Lord."

Felix's Nunna exchanged smiles with her friends, impressed by Father Salvador's respectful demeanour. The new priest stood silently at Father Constantine's side as the older priest conducted the mass, but when the time came for the sermon, he delivered a passionate call to help the less fortunate: "If we cannot help our fellow people, what other purpose do we have in this life? Especially on this day celebrating St. Francis of Assisi and his good deeds."

To the congregation, it was like a fresh light after years of the same dull words without action. But for Felix, he connected most with Father Salvador's childhood: "I was but an orphan on the streets, never knowing my mother or father, and losing every person who cared for me. But God took pity on me and showed me the light. The Church took me in. Saved me."

After the mass had ended, the fair began outside. Violinists and accordion players performed their old Konkani songs, with some of the crowd singing along, and stalls sold sweets and small toys. Despite what had happened the night before, Felix's father, perhaps feeling guilty for using the cane, gave his three boys money to spend. Felix found Clara, and with his father's money, bought them the kadio bodio they had been craving, along with the sugar-filled and snow-flake-shaped fulfuli. They ate their snacks watching Wagh Marea—who normally only visited the church for confession—secretly freshen his sugar-cane juice from the stand with a liberal splash of fenny.

A crowd had gathered around Father Salvador, and Miguel soon called Felix and his brothers over to their Nunna, who held her knee. He told them she was in pain and needed help home. Felix was going to volunteer to take her, but his father told Nicholas and Jacob to go.

"But the fair just started," Nicholas said.

"And why does Felix get to stay?" Jacob asked.

"Because I said so. You can both come back after. Now go."

As they walked away, Miguel gestured to Felix to join the line to meet Father Salvador; Felix knew his father had chosen him only because he'd already met the priest, but he couldn't help but feel more special than his brothers.

Meanwhile, Diego had joined the celebration, avoiding Wagh and tying his horse not far from Father Salvador's carriage and horse beside the church. The crowd parted to let Diego skip the line to meet Father Salvador, though he shook his countryman's hand for longer than normal and held his eyes inquisitively—almost suspiciously. Felix assumed that Diego was jealous of Father Salvador getting the attention he normally received.

The line inched forward, and Felix and Miguel finally had their turn.

"Felix, how are you? This is your father, I assume?"

"Yes." Felix was surprised that Father Salvador remembered

his name, and he looked up at his father to ensure that he'd noticed, too.

"Pleased to make your acquaintance," Father Salvador said, and shook hands with Miguel. "Your son was so kind to point me in the direction of the church yesterday."

The priest offered Miguel a cigarette from his pack and lit it with his silver lighter, and then asked Felix what he planned to do the rest of the day.

Miguel answered for him, "Hopefully not get into more trouble."

Felix looked at Father Salvador, embarrassed by his father's words. But the priest only laughed. "He couldn't have gotten into that much trouble."

"He spends too much time under the zamblam trees. What do you think about those trees? They say they're haunted."

"Oh, that's just rubbish."

Felix grinned, delighted the priest had taken his side.

Father Salvador continued: "As long as you have faith in our Heavenly Father, you should not worry about such things."

Miguel pressed further. "But has Father Constantine told you about the house at the top of the hill yet? The boy went there last night as well."

"That's another story. Felix, you must not go looking for evil." Father Salvador's tone turned severe and he put a hand on the boy's shoulder. "You must promise me not to go to this house again."

Felix was confused why he would say one superstition was nonsense and the other not, though he wanted to remain on Father's good side. But before Felix could promise, a horse neighed loudly nearby, interrupting them. They turned to see Father Salvador's horse stomping its feet and tugging at its tether. It had an erection and was staring at Diego's horse.

All eyes were drawn to the horse's rigid penis, engorged to the size of a man's arm.

"Bastard!" Father Salvador shouted, and rushed over to take the reins and direct the horse away.

People laughed, and Wagh Marea was quick to quip, "Someone forgot to tell the priest's horse he's supposed to be celibate."

Felix had never heard a priest swear before but was glad the distraction freed him from his father further embarrassing him. He slipped away and walked home alone.

In just a few short days, Father Salvador made an impression on the village, and the incident with the horse was overlooked. He visited families and offered his advice to anyone who asked. "Such a lovely young fellow," the older women said to each other. "Straight from God he was sent," others said, which might have had something to do with the fact that he had doubled the collection-plate money on the feast day.

By the following Sunday, it felt as though Father Salvador had been living in the community for years. That Sunday was also the anniversary of Felix's mother's death. Although Felix's family celebrated his birthday the following day, his actual day of birth had always been spent at home in mourning. Their only excursion was to attend mass, dressed entirely in black.

At mass, Clara and her family offered condolences to Felix and his. Felix hadn't felt the day's sadness until he saw Clara, as if seeing his close friend made him aware of what he had lost. When Clara hugged him and said, "I'm sorry for your loss," he thanked her and squeezed her tighter and longer than the rest of her family.

When it came time for Father Salvador's second sermon, the parishioners hushed one another and leaned forward in their seats.

"One day, just before mass, a young priest couldn't find the sermon he had prepared. He frantically looked through all of the drawers of his desk and dresser without any luck."

Felix enjoyed how Father Salvador brought the story to life by opening imaginary drawers.

Father continued: "The priest finally turned his head skyward, closed his eyes, and prayed to our Heavenly Father. He said, 'God, if you help me find my sermon, I swear to give up whisky for the rest of my life.' The young priest opened his eyes, looked down, and saw the sermon lying right in front of him on the dresser." Father Salvador paused to capture the parishioners' full engagement. "The young priest looked skyward and said to God, 'Never mind, I found it myself.'"

The congregation erupted in laughter. Felix couldn't remember a time he'd laughed like that in church. Though his father was not laughing: his jaw was clenched, his eyebrows furrowed in rage.

Back at home, as they had every year, Felix's family kept a vigil by the altar in their main room, with a single photo of his mother on display amid the lit candles and fresh garlands. They fasted during the day, and Felix's stomach grumbled as they worked their way through the rosary. But he welcomed this hunger, as if he deserved the discomfort and slight pain for having had any part in taking his mother away.

While his father and Nunna closed their eyes during the prayers, Felix caught his brothers playing tic-tac-toe. He tried to think loving thoughts of his mother, but the repetition of the prayers made it feel so impersonal. His father never shared any special stories or details about his mother—all they had was that one photo of her as a teenager, her shoulder-length hair parted down the middle. In the flickering candlelight, Felix stared at it now. His mother wasn't smiling but looked like she was about to. If only the picture had been taken a moment later.

As the evening angelus church bells rang, they ate only dal and rice for supper. Jacob and Nicholas licked their fingers, and Felix's Nunna said, "Hunger makes the best curry."

After the meal, Miguel went to place a glass bottle of holy water next to the picture on the altar, but realized he'd forgotten to have Father Salvador bless it.

Felix jumped at the chance to escape and volunteered to take it to the church. He fetched Clara, and together they made their way to the church in the waning light. As they neared the statue of St. Francis of Assisi, they heard the church bells ring out in rapid succession.

"Something must be wrong," Clara said, recognizing the call for help.

"Let's go check," said Felix.

They discovered Wagh Marea sitting on the church steps, rubbing his head. But before he could tell them what had happened, a rumble of horses approached from the village. Diego and a few other men on horseback galloped to the church entrance, kicking up a trail of red dust behind them. The riders came to a halt, and the dust clouded Felix's vision for a few moments.

Diego asked, "What happened?"

"Robbers," Wagh said.

Diego waited a few seconds, unaccustomed to such a short reply from Wagh. "What did they take?"

"They took Father Salvador and his horse and carriage and rode off. Raided the church, too. Took all the money from the collection, and as much gold and silver as they could carry. They tied up Father Constantine and the bell operator inside. I had to untie them."

"How many were there?" Diego asked.

"Just two. One fellow was big as a bear, though; the other one thin but strong." Wagh rubbed his swollen head. "And they took my bottle of fenny, too, and gave me a knock on the head with it. Bastards. It was a full bottle!"

"I don't care about your bottle, Wagh. Which way did they go?"

"The road down by the river."

"And you say they rode Father Salvador's carriage?"

"Yes. They came in on one horse but stole Father Salvador's horse and carriage with him inside."

Diego talked with his fellow riders and told Wagh to stay at the church, then turned to Felix and Clara. "Go home. This isn't the time for children to be out," he said, before riding off with the others down the road by the river.

As Felix and Clara walked away from the church, Wagh's description of the robbers resonated in Felix's mind: *one big, one thin.* He grabbed Clara's shoulder and said, "I think I know where they're going."

"Who?"

"The robbers—I saw them behind the house at the top of the hill. We have to help Father Salvador."

Moonlight shone over the vine-covered house and the expansive zamblam tree as Felix and Clara approached, slightly out of breath after climbing the hill. Along the way, Felix had pocketed stones for his slingshot, switching the bottle of holy water from one hand to the other.

The stone that Felix's brothers had used to block the front door was still there, and Clara found the dropped flashlight and tested it. The beam illuminated a man striding toward them from the hill path.

"Felix!" cried this figure—Miguel. "What are you doing here? As soon as I heard the bells I knew I shouldn't have let you out. I sent your brothers to the church, but something told me I'd find you here. You haven't learned your lesson. And worse, you've brought Clara again."

"There's been a robbery at the church, and I saw the robbers here the other night. And they've kidnapped Father Salvador."

Felix watched his father's face change briefly from anger to concern, but then Miguel glanced up at the old house, staring at it as if it had just appeared. Then he noticed the giant zam-blam tree he'd hurried right past. "We need to get away from this cursed place," he said, his voice trembling. "God will take care of the priest."

But it was too late—the horses and carriage came thundering onto the property. The slender man dismounted from the lead horse, and the bear-sized man and Father Salvador hopped down from the carriage. The priest wasn't tied up. In fact, he carried a rifle, which hung over his shoulder instead of being pointed at the pair of robbers.

Clara grabbed Felix's hand and squeezed. In her other hand she accidentally flicked the flashlight off, then clutched it to her chest and looked up at the men.

"What have we got here?" asked the bigger man, who had the thickest arms Felix had ever seen.

The skinny man shook Wagh's bottle of fenny at Miguel. "You chose the wrong night to come here."

Led by Father Salvador, the trio of robbers approached.

"God will protect us," Miguel whispered to no one in particular.

Father Salvador stood before Felix. "Does anyone know you're here, son?"

"Diego is on his way," Felix tried, but his shaking voice betrayed him.

Father Salvador took out a cigarette and lit it with his silver lighter. "Ah, but they've gone chasing us in the complete opposite direction." He drew a long puff and exhaled. "Now, the question is, what can we do about this situation?"

"God will protect us," Miguel repeated.

Father Salvador turned to the massive man. "Ox?"

"Up to you, boss," he said.

"Gustavo?"

The skinny man laughed, then opened the bottle of alcohol. He took a swig and coughed. "Whoa, that's strong!"

"How could you?" Clara spoke up to Salvador, surprising Felix. "Pretending to be a priest. You're a disgrace!"

"I may have presented myself in a certain manner," Salvador said. "But everyone in the village made a choice to believe me. I think the smaller the village, the more it *needs to believe* that some people are closer to God than others. Simply so they have a scale on which to place themselves. Now, what's more disgraceful?"

Salvador took a final drag of his cigarette and exhaled the smoke in one long plume. He ground out the cigarette with his foot, walked over to Felix, and removed the bottle of holy water from his hands. Felix watched helplessly as Salvador opened the cap of holy water and drank the bottle empty.

Miguel repeated, "God will protect us."

Felix clenched his fists. "Stop saying that!" He stared at Salvador with contempt and touched the pocket that held his slingshot. But, glancing at the rifle again, he didn't reach for it.

Salvador wiped his mouth, said, "It's just water," and tossed the empty bottle to the ground. Then he walked over to Gustavo and took the bottle of fenny. "And this is just alcohol." He gave it a sniff but didn't drink it. "Now, unfortunately we can't let you three go and tell my secret to the world." Salvador walked up to the house and began splashing the alcohol on the dry vines covering the outside walls. When it was empty, he threw the bottle on the roof, where it shattered. Then he motioned to his partners. "Put them in the house."

Gustavo took the flashlight from Clara and tossed it to the ground. He grabbed Felix and Clara by the arms and brought them to the door. Ox handled Miguel as easily as his accomplice did the children, and with one hand moved the stone away from the door so they could push their captives inside.

The closing door brought darkness upon them.

"I told you not to come here," said Miguel. But he sounded feeble now.

Felix tried to open the door, but Ox had rolled the stone back in place and it wouldn't budge. In the dark, he found Clara's hand and they pulled each other close.

"Oh, Rosetta, why did you leave me?" Felix's father cried.

From outside came a crackling sound.

"They're lighting the house on fire!" Clara shouted.

But Felix's father only continued. "I knew this child would be the death of me. It wasn't enough he took you away from me."

Felix could smell smoke. Seething, he shouted back at his dad, "It's not my fault Mom died!"

The flames were devouring the dry vines that covered the house. The whooshes and crackles of the fire grew louder and the spaces between the tiles glowed. But down the hallway, through the back kitchen, shone a different kind of paler light. Moonlight.

Still holding Clara's hand, Felix told her, "I know a way out."

Felix's father again cried, "Rosetta!"

Felix took two steps down the hallway but turned back. He found his father's hand and pulled him to his feet. They ran toward the backroom. The old roof tiles rattled and began to crack and fall, shattering on the floor around them.

Felix jumped out the window first, then helped Clara out. His father stood there, framed in the window of the burning house. For a moment Felix wondered if he didn't want to be rescued.

But then he, too, came through the window.

The *twang* started up somewhere in the darkness, but Felix wasn't going to run this time. He led his father and Clara around the side of the burning house to the zamblam tree, where they hid.

"We'll stay here until they leave," Miguel whispered.

In the hellish glow of the blaze, Felix could see the robbers at the top of the hill. Salvador and Ox were in the carriage and Gustavo was tethering the horses.

The banging grew in intensity. Clara and Felix's father looked from side to side and up and down to try to locate its source, crouching closer to the tree when they couldn't. But the sound gave Felix strength. He saw that the noise was making Salvador's white horse restless, but Gustavo held its reins tight to keep from losing control. From his vantage point he could just make out the horse's balls hanging between its legs.

Despite Miguel and Clara calling him back, Felix crept out from behind the zamblam tree. At a crouch, he moved as close as he could and took the slingshot and a stone from his pocket. He placed the stone in the brace and pulled it back, aiming, waiting. The horse's leg and tail were in the way, and he worried he'd be seen in the fire's light. But then the horse shifted its position, and Felix's target loomed into view.

He fired.

The white horse roared and bucked, knocking the carriage toward the slope of the hill. As it began to roll backward, the horses bolted in the opposite direction, dragging Gustavo, tangled in the reins and screaming, onto the road to Mapusa. The carriage, heavy with gold and silver and men, crested the hill, teetered for a moment, then went flying downward.

Another banging sound rang out as Miguel peeked out from

behind the tree and called Felix over again. Felix ignored him, running to the top of the hill to watch the carriage barrelling toward the cemetery. For a moment he lost sight of it in the dark, but then a tremendous crash came from below. And silence.

1994

Carriers

Burlington, Ontario, Canada:

"Look at that one, he's got a big butt," said my sister.

"Ants don't have butts, Ally. It's called an abdomen."

"How can they not have butts?"

"I don't know." I knew an explanation would bring another endless string of questions.

We'd been squatting on the sidewalk for five minutes, our eyes fixed on the two lines of ants trailing to and from someone's dropped Popsicle. The Popsicle had melted, and the stick lay in a pool of pink sugar that the ants sucked up and carried away. Because of the weight, the line of ants that took away the sweet liquid moved more slowly than the line that arrived.

I liked ants. They always seemed to be working on something. A display at the Science Centre had an anthill with small plastic windows to provide glimpses into their lives. There was so much activity going on in the passageways and chambers, the ants constantly at work and in motion.

"Look, Aiden, those two are fighting!" Ally said, pointing. Two ants had broken off from the rest to wrestle each other. We watched them fight until one ant was decapitated and dragged away. "Why did he do that?" she asked.

I stood. "C'mon, we should get going."

I took two pieces of cinnamon gum from my fanny pack and gave one to Ally, getting ready for Chrissy's house—she was a girl in my class I didn't like. Then I counted the money we'd collected so far. "Think we can get twenty-five more dollars? I need twelve to get my new baseball glove before the tournament."

"Twenty-five dollars!" Ally said, chewing her gum. "That'll be tough the second time around."

She took out the notebook and opened it to the last lined page. In the neatly written column for April were all the house numbers that regularly paid but we hadn't collected from yet. The *Post* was our town's community newspaper, and most of the sixty houses we delivered to gave us a small tip every month— our spending money. Dad took the pennies-per-paper the *Post* paid us as a salary and put it into savings bonds each year. "For your university," he said. University seemed too far away to be real, but Dad always said it with a smile. He once showed us Mom's and his very first bank statement from when they came to Canada. Ally and I took the folded pages from their original envelope and read the names, Felix A. Pinto and Clara M. Pinto, and the balance of just thirty dollars. Dad told us, "And we had to borrow that thirty dollars, too. At that time you were only allowed to bring ten dollars out of India, and that went in the first days."

Ally and I walked along the sidewalk, following our regular route to houses with big garages and front lawns. We only went to the houses that paid when we collected for the month, and learned that Sunday, around five, was the best time to catch people at home. We always went together, because people tipped better when there were two of us.

None of the other kids in my class had jobs, but my best friend Johnny had an older brother who did papers, too. He sometimes just threw his whole stack in the dumpster behind the convenience store. But we always delivered our papers on time. A truck came to our house three times a week to drop off big bundles of newspapers and flyers. We assembled them as fast as we could and became expert shoppers in the process—we flipped through the glossy inserts from every store and spotted the sales.

The other day my sister had proudly told my father, "Basmati rice for three forty-nine."

"Oh, that's a very good price," he answered. He usually helped us assemble the papers after work but had to take a nap right after.

"Ice cream's on sale for a dollar forty-nine, too," I added, trying my luck.

We had a system for delivering papers. We'd memorize the house numbers, load up the metal wire buggy, and each take a side of the street. We'd then meet at the end with ink-stained hands in front of Chrissy's house to spit our gum onto the sidewalk. When we got home, Mom made us wash our hands the moment we stepped inside so we didn't get fingerprints all over the white walls. Black soapy bubbles, and we were done.

I blew a bubble with my gum and checked the count with Ally—after the first five houses, we'd collected only six dollars. We approached number 656 hoping the Sheppards were home. Mr. and Mrs. Sheppard were always nice to us, and Mr. Sheppard was so interesting. He was the only man I knew who had a long grey ponytail, and it seemed like every time we saw him he'd just come back from playing hockey, or ice fishing, or camping or hiking up north with Mrs. Sheppard.

We walked past the Volkswagen in the driveway, onto the porch, and knocked on the door. We heard movement inside the house, and through the pane of blurred glass next to the door we saw a figure coming down the stairs.

Mr. Sheppard opened the door, wearing what he always wore: blue jeans and a black T-shirt, his ponytail hanging down the back, and a thick wooden pipe in his mouth.

Ally said, "Hi, we're collecting for the *Post*."

"Of course, come on in and I'll see what I can scrounge up."

Fruity-smelling smoke trailed behind Mr. Sheppard as we followed him inside. Mom had told us not to go into people's homes, but we sometimes did, anyway.

"You kids aren't thirsty, are you?" he called from the kitchen.

"No thank you. We're fine," I said back, unsure if he heard me.

My eyes darted around the hallway and living room, over the snowshoes in the corner, the porcelain dog next to the reclining chair, the long piece of driftwood and mason jar filled with seashells and smooth stones on top of the coffee table, before settling on a big framed painting hanging above the couch. The painting was of a lake at sunset with evergreens all around, and the sky and water were pink. Mr. Sheppard had told us his grandfather had painted it. It made me want a picture like that in our house, but I only had one grandparent left, and he was in India.

Mr. Sheppard returned a few moments later, grinning around his pipe. "Well, I only got a ten, but here you go," he said, and handed Ally the bill.

She gave the ten to me, and I folded it into the fanny pack. Mr. Sheppard must have still been in a good mood. Just last week his picture had been in the paper beside an article about him trying to stop the city from building new houses by the creek. We had given him all the extra copies we had of that day's paper. He said he was going to frame the article.

46

"Now, that money is for you two, do you understand?" he said. "I don't want any of that going to the *Post*."

We promised him we would keep the money, and said thank you before we headed out the door.

After Mr. Sheppard's, I thought for sure we'd get enough to buy my baseball glove. A lot of other families weren't home, though, and by the time we reached the last house—Chrissy's—we were still four dollars short. The sun was not so high anymore. I thought of my old baseball glove, which the ball sometimes went right through.

As we approached the house, I saw the blotches of gum on the sidewalk. Chrissy had been in my class since kindergarten. Every year we competed for the best grades. Whenever we got a test back, she would come over to my desk and compare marks. She kept quiet if I got a better score than her, but if she scored higher, she always said, "I beat you." But that's not why I didn't like her. At the bake sale last year, I'd brought in Kulkuls. My family usually only made the sweet at Christmas, but it was my mom's idea to make them the Saturday before the sale. Most kids brought in cookies, cakes, and frosted muffins topped with Smarties happy faces, and my teacher and the other parents loved how the Kulkuls weren't so sugary and had more of a spicy-sweet taste.

When my teacher asked how they were made, I began to explain how we rolled small pieces of dough on a comb to make the shape of a shell.

Chrissy interrupted. "That's disgusting!"

I tried to tell her it was a brand-new comb that we boiled first and just used to get the pattern, but it didn't work. She told everyone my dessert was made with a comb and had hair inside. None of the kids would try one after that. Chrissy's mom had brought in a giant gingerbread house that everyone loved. She gave each kid a gingerbread man, too. Mine was missing an icing eye, and also went uneaten.

After that, we still delivered the paper to Chrissy's house, but stopped collecting from her. Every time I passed her house, I made sure no one was looking and spat out my gum on the sidewalk. After a while, the gum got flattened and dirty, and turned black. Ally had started joining me, too, when I told her the gum-spitting was non-violent resistance. When we were younger and Mom had told us about Gandhi, we imagined an Indian Hercules, strong and powerful. We were shocked when we finally saw a photo of him. This skinny bald man with thick glasses couldn't possibly be the man who had freed India from the British. "His power," our mother told us, "came from within."

Ally was about to spit her gum out on Chrissy's sidewalk, and I told her to wait. "Let's try this house."

"I thought she was mean to you?"

"I know, but they pay every time we go. And I need that glove."

As we were deciding in front of Chrissy's house, with its perfect grass and double garage, a BMW pulled into the driveway. Chrissy and her mom got out.

"Hi! How are you kids? Are you collecting?" Chrissy's mom looked like Barbie and carried a shiny shopping bag in each hand.

"Yes, for the *Post*," Ally managed to say.

I tried to cover the gum spots with my shoe.

"Well, come on inside and I'll check if I have any cash."

Chrissy wore a Girl Guides uniform with a sash full of badges. She said, "Hey," as she passed by and our eyes met. I tried to hide my gum under my tongue, but Ally was still chewing away.

I said, "Hey," but it didn't sound right.

We followed her up the steps and into her house. There was a dining room to the left of the foyer, a spiral staircase to the right, and a long hallway straight ahead with a hardwood floor. We stood next to a glass table with a vase filled with dried flowers. My mom didn't like flowers that were fake or plants that weren't alive. She had potted versions of her favourites from back home: a rubber plant, a small palm tree, and pink bougainvilleas that she kept outside in the summer to flower. I thought they looked better than dried flowers, too.

Chrissy went up the stairs, and her mom put her shopping bags on the dining table. When she closed the glass doors on her way out of the dining room, I thought of the beaded curtains that separated our family room and hallway. Ally and I always tried to limbo underneath them, or part their way with the least movement and noise.

Chrissy's mom returned with her purse, but shouted out, "Dad?" before she opened it. "Dad? Did you eat the food I left out?"

An old man appeared at the end of the hallway and stared at us. He wore a grey wool sweater and had white hair and stubble on his face.

The phone rang, and Chrissy's mom said to us, "Oh, just a sec, kids." She put her purse on the ground and ran into another room.

Ally tugged my shirt and gave me a look like she was uncomfortable. I mouthed, *Wait*. It would look weird if we just left. But then the old man started shuffling slowly toward us.

I heard Chrissy's mom say hello three times, each time slower than the last, before she finally hung up.

"Must have been a wrong number," she said as she returned, and picked her purse off the floor. We watched her dig around in it for a while.

"Jeez, I've got no cash on me," she said. "Just hold on another minute and let me see if I have anything upstairs."

All the flavour in my gum had gone and it was getting harder to chew. And the old man was getting closer to us. He held his backside as he walked. And he was crying silently, tears rolling down his wrinkled face.

Then I noticed the smell. I turned to Ally, who was looking more and more nervous.

Before either of us could speak, the front door opened and Chrissy's dad walked in. He wore a suit and had a leather bag slung over his shoulder like he'd just returned from work—strange on a Sunday.

"Jennifer!" he shouted, ignoring us. "Did Richard call?"

Chrissy's mom came halfway down the stairs. "Someone just called, but they didn't say anything."

"I've got to give him a call." He walked past us without a word or a nod but stopped before he reached the stairs.

"Jesus Christ, what is that smell?"

The old man said in a quiet voice, "I had an accident."

Chrissy's mom's face dropped. She took half a step downstairs, but then paused and simply told him to go wait in the washroom.

"I'm sorry, I don't know what happened," the old man whispered. His face was scrunched up like he was in pain, and it made me feel like I was the one who had the accident. He shuffled back down the hallway.

"This is what I come home to?" Chrissy's father stomped up the stairs. "Jen, we're putting him in a home."

"I'm not putting my father in a home." She followed him up and into a room we couldn't see, but we could still hear them.

"Then what do you want to do?" said Chrissy's dad. "And where were you all day, anyway?"

"Grocery shopping, pharmacy, florist, Chrissy's piano lessons, and Girl Guides. If you weren't at work all the time, you'd know this."

"My work pays for all those things, Jennifer. And right now I'm busy. I need to make a call."

"You're always busy. Did you spend today with that woman again?"

"She's my *client*, for fuck's sake!"

I heard what I thought was a stomp on the floor; it rumbled through the house.

Ally tugged at my shirt again, harder this time. She didn't speak, but her eyes were afraid. Our parents argued sometimes but never like that.

As we turned to go, Chrissy came down the stairs and stopped when she saw we were still there. She was stuck on that step for a few seconds, her parents arguing behind her.

"Mom." Chrissy ran back upstairs. "Mom! The paperboys are still downstairs."

Ally's face scrunched; she hated being called a paper*boy*.

"Just tell them to come back another time, Chrissy."

A door slammed upstairs, and the shouting started again.

A few seconds passed before Chrissy came back down. I was expecting her to tell us what we had just heard, about coming back another time.

"You'll wait forever for money, won't you?" she said.

I didn't say anything to her and neither did Ally, but when I shook my head, our eyes met, and she turned away and ran back upstairs.

Outside, with the door closed behind us, we breathed deeply. It had felt like Chrissy's house was running out of air.

Down on the sidewalk were the gum spots. As we walked over them, I swallowed the dry, hardened gum in my mouth—it caught in my throat before going down.

Ally was looking at me. She spoke softly: "I can lend you the money for the glove from my share."

I thanked her, but she just nodded, spat her gum out on the sidewalk, and turned to go. I glanced at the house and followed her with a chuckle, walking home slowly with the weight of all that we carried.

Birds of a Feather

For some reason you could never just *play* when Cory was around. There was always an objective. He had moved into Johnny's house only two weeks before, but my summer break had gotten so much worse since.

Johnny Long was my best friend. He'd lived across the street since forever. The day after we'd moved into our townhouse, he told me his name was "long johns" backwards and his house was the one with the crab-apple tree out front. We played cards and drank root beer that day. Since then, he's rung our doorbell every day after school and every morning in the summer. Although since Cory arrived, I'd become the one who called on him.

Johnny and I were playing catch in his backyard one day when Cory joined us. He leaned against the tall wooden post where Johnny's dad had hung a hummingbird feeder. I liked to watch the tiny birds hover and dart through the air, their wings flapping so fast they were invisible. They'd sip the sweet red liquid, then disappear. But today there were none because

Cory shook the post. Once he'd got bored of that, he suggested we go light a fire in the field behind our houses.

"Don't worry, kids," he said, "I'll bring some water."

He held up an old Coke can and gave it a slight shake. I hated when he called us "kids." We were only a year and a half younger than Cory, who was twelve, but he acted like he'd already learned how crappy life could get and treated anyone who thought otherwise like they were kidding themselves. I felt sorry for him sometimes. My mom had told me to be extra nice to him while he was here. "It'll do him wonders being in a good home out of the big city," she'd said. I wasn't so sure.

To get to the field, we took a path only a child could have carved: no roads, lots of shortcuts, and past any obstacles along the way. The first step was the creek. We crossed on wobbly stones just close enough to jump from one to the next. In the spring, the creek was full of spawning fish trying to get upstream. Johnny and I once caught two hundred suckers in a single day. We just picked them out of the water with our bare hands, then dropped them back in before they drank too much air. You'd need to use a net to get any fish now. Cory caught one when he first came, but he bashed it with a stone, then a brick, and left us with the mess.

I trailed behind Johnny. We both followed Cory. The chain on his wallet jangled with each step, and the smell from his lit cigarette surrounded him. He exhaled the smoke from his nose like a dragon, and every so often he blew smoke rings up into the air.

A long chain-link fence separated us from the field; to get over it we climbed the old willow tree. I loved that tree. Its giant trunk swallowed up the fence like it was nothing. Chain-links just disappeared into the bark. I wondered how it had grown like that, and wished I could have watched it happen with one of those time-lapse cameras. From the top branches, we could see the fence stretched out in a straight line in both directions. Johnny and I used to pretend we were sentry guards at some important border crossing. Today we still swung down from the tree's long hair, but Cory just jumped down from the branch and stormed past it.

As we walked, Cory told us stories of the foster homes he'd been in, and how he'd hitchhiked to Toronto. He claimed to be an atheist. I'd heard other people say they didn't believe in God, but Cory was the first I thought was telling the truth. As we walked, he said, "Any good in this world is nothing versus all the shitty things that happen. You guys, me, we're all going to get caught in the system in the end. Nothing we can do about it."

We passed the spot in the field where Johnny and I had gotten stuck while walking in the mud last spring. One of us could have saved our new white socks if the other had gone for help, but we both left our tall rubber boots behind instead. We hung our mud-soaked socks on the fence near the willow tree, hoping the rain would clean them. It didn't rain, though, and they turned stiff, like boomerangs that broke on the first throw. I didn't remind Johnny of it this time because Cory was with us. The sun had baked the whole place dry now, anyway.

Johnny asked Cory if he'd brought his switchblade, and he stopped beneath the tall evergreens to take it out and show us. It had a black handle and a shiny-sharp edge, and Mrs. Long didn't know about it.

"I always carry it just in case I run into the old man."

Johnny had already warned me not to ask about Cory's mother. But Cory talked about what he'd do to his father all the time. He actually showed us then, approaching a pine tree with a trunk as thick as a man. Cory put one arm around its imaginary shoulder. "Hey, Pops! Long time no see!" His other hand, down by his side, held the switchblade. With one quick upward motion he thrust the blade into the bark's belly. "How do you like that, old man?"

I looked away, scared. Up in the sky, I spotted the hawk. It slowly soared across the sky with brown-and-white wings stretched wide; there was an ease in its glide and glance for prey.

"Johnny, there's the hawk again," I said, pointing.

Johnny looked up and asked Cory, "Think he's hunting?"

"Maybe," Cory said. He watched the hawk with a hand raised to block the sun. "I would love to fly that high, you could go anywhere you want." I was surprised Cory said this, and not something about the hawk's sharp claws and beak and tearing animals to pieces.

Johnny and I had seen the hawk land in the tall evergreen trees a few times and guessed that that must be where it nested. From a nature program, I'd learned that hummingbirds make their nests in the same trees as hawks. Hawks attacked other birds, but hummingbirds were too small. And being so close to a top predator meant the hummingbirds were safe from squirrels and rodents. I wondered if they were affected by the hawk's presence. Or was it the other way around? Maybe nature brought them together on purpose.

Cory stopped us in the field and said, "It's as good a spot as any."

We were a few hundred feet from the tall evergreens, and in the other direction sat a lone model home. The show house had popped up almost overnight and looked out of place in the field. My dad had said one day there would be a sea of houses here.

"Think they can see us?" I pointed to the house.

Cory barely glanced over his shoulder. "Fuck 'em." It made me smile because I didn't like that house either; they were trying to take our field away. To them the field looked empty, but they were wrong.

"Grab anything that will burn," Cory commanded.

Johnny and I collected dead grass, large and small sticks, and a few fallen branches. Everything was so dry this time of year, it was easy. We made a monster of a pile.

Cory watched us and smoked. It seemed like we'd been doing everything he ordered ever since he came. The previous week at the outdoor pool, Cory had brought a girl with blond hair and braces into the family change room and made us keep watch outside. She came out first, pale, with a single tear rolling down her cheek. When we asked Cory what he'd done, the only answer we got was, "Wholesome things."

I watched Cory tear a piece of cardboard from his cigarette pack and light it. He placed it at the bottom of the mountain we'd made, then picked up his Coke can and stepped back.

For the first few seconds the fire was lovely; it was just grasping at life. I had never seen a fire uncaged like that. The flame burned bright yellow as it grew.

"It's getting bigger," I said, taking a step back.

Johnny looked to Cory, who was like a statue watching the fire.

When the fire let out its first roar, I knew we were in trouble. I couldn't turn away, though; part of me wanted to see the fire grow.

"Maybe we should put some water on it?" Johnny asked Cory.

Cory held out the Coke can. Johnny took it and stretched his arm out to tilt it over the fire. Water tumbled out and sizzled below with each shake, but the can couldn't have been more than half-full.

I tried to kick dirt on the fire, but it was full of dried grass and plants, and I ended up just providing more fuel.

"I'm going to go get some more water," Johnny shouted,

holding up the can. He ran a few yards before he stopped and looked back at me alone with Cory and the fire, then came back, standing by my side.

Cory finally moved. The fire was half his height, but he took a few steps closer, dropped his shorts, and started to pee. The smell of urine filled the air. The fire hissed, but took only a few moments to recover. It roared back with twice the life, as if insulted by what Cory had just done.

"You little bitches! Don't just stand there and stare at my cock!" He waited for a response, but we were stuck in our places like we had been in the mud.

The fire was taller than us now. Grey smoke and orange embers raced one another toward the sky. The air surrounding the fire was a blur, like a street on a hot day, and waves of heat came off the blaze onto our faces. The earth all around us glowed and crackled.

I realized Cory was moving toward us. My eyes followed his arm down to his hand, which was clenched tight around his switchblade. Smaller flames spread between us, but all I could see was that blade. And Cory was pointing it at us now, the fire reflected in his eyes.

"Either of you say a word about this and I'll take you down with me. You'll both be sent to juvie till you're old enough to go to a real jail. And when you get out, your parents won't want anything to do with you."

Then the smoke surged, forcing me to turn away and cough.

"Do you hear me?" Cory screamed.

I felt a hand on my shoulder. Johnny. His face determined. "We gotta go."

And we ran. As fast as we could.

I didn't look back until we were up in the willow tree again. Johnny and I perched there, out of breath, as the smoke rose high in the distance, now dark and thick. The fire must have gotten hold of something big—the model home, I realized. I couldn't tell if it had reached the tall evergreens. I hoped the hawk had escaped. I could hear bird cries all around but couldn't pick it out of the many in the air, flying away.

1995

Picking Trilliums

Only when we're the last ones left on the bus ride home does Aiden talk to me. Between bumps that send us bouncing slightly in our seats he turns to me and asks, "Why were you late today, Ally?"

"Tommy Groh wanted to see my feet," I say.

"And why did that make you late?" Aiden takes an orange, leftover from lunch, out of his bag. He bites it with his bottom teeth to break the skin and starts peeling it.

"Ms. Bisset made me dust the chalk brushes before I left," I tell him, and hold my hands up as proof. They're dried white by the chalk, like I've switched hands with an old person. I rest them at my sides so I don't get chalk on my skirt.

"But *why* did your teacher keep you?" Aiden peels the orange skin off in a spiral, like a pig's tail. He always tries to take the whole thing off in one go.

"Tommy wouldn't stop bothering me, so I kicked him in the stomach." I think my brother will be happy that I've stuck up for myself, but he stops peeling the orange and shakes his head.

"Ally, you're not going to make any new friends if you go around kicking people."

"But it's not my fault! That meanie kept asking me if my toes were brown, too. And I don't want to be Tommy's friend, anyway."

It isn't fair—I used to have a best friend named Sara in my class. She had a grey cat named Smoke, and she liked dill pickle chips, too. But she moved away when her dad got a new job in Peterborough. I still don't know where that is. Everyone says it isn't far, but I haven't seen her since.

A few weeks later we got Tommy Groh in our class.

"Tommy's probably only curious," says Aiden. "Next time tell him your feet are the same colour as the rest of you." Aiden removes the whole orange peel, forms it into its original shape, and puts it back in his lunch bag. He splits the orange in two and offers me half.

I shake my head, then pick at a piece of dark green sticky tape that covers a hole in the back of the seat ahead of us. "You said you'd protect me."

"I will," Aiden says quickly, with orange slices in his mouth. He swallows and adds, "I'll talk to Tommy tomorrow."

"Tomorrow's our field trip."

"Then the day after."

I nod my head, feeling better. "Did anyone ever ask to see your feet when you were in Grade 2?" I ask.

"Worse. The boys asked what colour my you-know-what was." He points at his crotch. "And the girls, the girls wanted to feel my soft brown ears." Aiden smiles his slow smile, like honey being poured. It's impossible not to smile with him. "And don't worry, Ally-cat, I won't tell Mom. We'll just rinse your hands with the garden hose before we go inside."

I forgot about Mom. I'd be in big trouble at home if I got in small trouble at school. She always puts our education first. It's a good thing she won't find out tonight, or she might not let me go on my field trip tomorrow. I'll tell her after that. I think she'll be on my side, anyway—she was last time something like this happened. It was during Black History Month when we learned about Rosa Parks not sitting at the back of the bus. I found it strange how she wanted to sit at the front; everyone I know fights for a spot at the back of the bus.

I asked Ms. Bisset, "Where would I sit on the bus back then?"

"I don't know," she snapped. "It's not an appropriate question."

When I told Mom, she said it was a perfectly fine question, and she agreed with me that I'd probably sit somewhere in the middle, like I do now.

The Royal Botanical Gardens are only a short bus ride from our school, but so different from the concrete schoolyard. Everywhere giant trees and plants are coming to life. Our class spends most of the morning inside the greenhouses—the air is wet and there are shiny-leafed plants from all around the world, some with flowers as bright and colourful as saris.

Then it's lunch. I avoid sitting near Tommy because of what happened yesterday, and because Mom packed me a brown paper bag with a juice box and two chapatis with peanut butter. "East meets West," she said. Almost everyone else has white-bread sandwiches. Chapatis are tastier, but sometimes I wish I had the same lunch so I wouldn't have to explain what I was eating. Natalie Dibben is the one who asks me about it today. She's my buddy for the trip, and her mom brought her a special lunch, too. Natalie always tells people she's different because she has diabetes, and she shows everyone her lunch instead of keeping it hidden like me.

After lunch we are led on a nature walk through the forest trails. I've worn my pink rubber boots because Mom said it might rain. Our guide points out things along the way as she leads the group; she's wearing a dark green windbreaker and has three earrings in each ear. My teacher, Ms. Bisset, is at the back of the line chatting with Mrs. Dibben, who's a nurse and works night shifts, so she can usually come on our trips to help supervise. I wish my mom could get time off work one day to come, too.

The plump, grey clouds above look ready to burst, but the sun peeks out every once in a while. I hear birds chirping in the trees but can't spot any because Natalie keeps distracting me.

"Do you like my medic alert?" she holds up her arm, showing the bracelet off like it's diamond jewellery.

"It's nice," I say.

"How many needles have *you* had?"

I shrug.

"I've taken so many needles, they don't even hurt anymore."

Needles are scary. I could never imagine them not hurting. When I think of them, a circus starts in my stomach.

We stop walking, surrounded by tall trees that show only small pieces of sky. Our guide pulls a big bag of birdseed from her knapsack. She carefully pours little piles of seed into our hands, one by one. Everyone crowds around her and wants to be the first to get theirs, including Tommy. I wait until he's moved on to get my seeds.

"Spread out into a circle," our guide says. "Hold your hands very still and they will come and get it."

Small birds appear from the forest like magic. They come closer, down to lower branches, then right into the hands of my classmates. Some of the students laugh out loud, a few scream and drop the seed on the ground, and others stare silently. But no birds land in my hands. I'm in the same circle and I hold my hands as still as I can, but none come.

Ms. Bisset begins to gather students to continue along the

trail. I tell her I haven't fed any birds yet. She gives me a look.

"I can stay behind with Ally until she gets one." It's Mrs. Dibben, Natalie's mom.

"Oh, you don't have to do that," Ms. Bisset says.

"It's no problem. I'd be glad to."

"Alright, then. Ally, what do you say to Mrs. Dibben?"

"Thank you," I say. I could have hugged Mrs. Dibben. I like her much better than Natalie.

Tommy approaches Ms. Bisset and says, "I didn't get any birds either."

I don't blame the birds for not wanting to land in Tommy's hands—he'd probably try and catch them. I can't understand why the birds wouldn't come into *my* hands, though. Maybe they can still smell the chalk from yesterday. But I washed my hands well. Plus I'm not even sure birds can smell.

"Okay. You can stay behind as well," says Ms. Bisset. "We'll have to switch partners. Tommy, you're now with Ally, and Natalie, you go with Ryan."

The rest of my class follows the guide down the trail while Tommy and I wait to see if we'll have more luck with the birds. Mrs. Dibben tells us to stretch out our arms as far away from us as we can and be very quiet. My hands are cupped tight to try and hold them still. I worry the birds are no longer hungry. But then one lands on the tips of my fingers. It's small with brown feathers on its back and lighter ones on its tummy. The bird has a short beak and black eyes that stare at me for just a second, as if asking first. Its feet prick my fingers, but they are too light to hurt. The bird dives in to eat the seed, but soon pops back up to stop and look around, its head moving from side to side. It looks delicate. My dad sometimes says I eat like a bird. He says I get distracted easily and sit with half a bum on my chair, ready to run if the doorbell or phone rings.

One more nibble and the bird takes off into the trees. I brush my hands together and let the few remaining seeds fall to the ground. Then I put my hands back in the pockets of my sweater and look over at Tommy. He's standing very still with his hands cupped together. He has two birds nibbling at the seed and isn't trying to kill them. Mrs. Dibben gives me a wink—but I've spotted something: trilliums.

They sit next to the path waiting to be noticed, like they've chosen a bad spot in hide-and-go-seek. Once you see them, you can't miss them, bright white on the forest floor and appearing secretly, like the birds.

"Oh, I love trilliums," says Mrs. Dibben. "A sure sign of spring. Do you kids know it's against the law to pick them?"

"Really?" says Tommy.

"Really," says Mrs. Dibben. "Picking the flower does awful damage to the plant. It can take a long time before it regrows, if it does at all. The only time it's acceptable is if you're going to transplant them. I tried it once. I put one in my front yard, but it just wouldn't take. They don't like the direct sunlight. I guess that's why you have to come out here and see them."

"Mrs. Dibben?" I say.

"Yes, sweetie."

"My mom told me that trilliums are angels. God sends them down to see the world first from the ground up. And they can only get their wings after they've been trilliums. But if they get picked, they can't make it back up to heaven."

"Little angels," says Mrs. Dibben. "Ally, tell your mother that's a lovely story."

Before I can answer, Ms. Bisset comes running down the path, screaming.

"Mrs. Dibben!" Her face is red. "Natalie's had an attack! She's passed out farther up the trail."

I see Mrs. Dibben's face change as she shifts gears like she must at the hospital when a patient comes in. "I'm on my way," she says.

"Ally, Tommy—stay right here on the trail," Ms. Bisset tells us. "I'm going to run and call 911."

The two women run off in opposite directions down the trail. I want to go with Mrs. Dibben. Adults always think they can run faster than kids, but I can run like the wind. Last summer I knocked out one of my baby teeth when I tripped over a groundhog hole running my fastest. Our doctor said I ran so fast, the ground couldn't keep up. I wonder if they'll take Natalie to the hospital. Maybe if she hadn't talked so much about her diabetes it wouldn't have happened. That's wrong. I hope she'll be okay.

I can't see my teacher or Mrs. Dibben anymore and I notice how quiet the forest has become. I turn to Tommy. He's stepped off the trail and is creeping toward the flowers. "What are you doing?"

"Nothing." He crouches down beside one of the trilliums and puts his hands around it.

"Stop it!" I yell.

"Make me."

I follow Tommy into the forest. But I'm too late: he plucks the trillium flower from its leaves. I can't believe what I've just seen. I want to cry.

"Here you go." Tommy holds the flower out for me, like I'm supposed to take it.

I'm confused why he's giving it to me, and still upset. "I don't want it."

"I thought girls liked flowers."

"I like them in the ground."

Tommy just tosses the flower to the forest floor.

"I'm going to tell." As soon as I say this, he pushes me to the ground. I don't see it coming and land on my elbows and bum.

"That's for kicking me yesterday," he says.

The damp leaves are soaking into me, but I just lie there. Tommy grabs one of my pink rubber boots and pulls. He wrestles it off my foot and throws it behind him, then yanks my sock off and does the same with it. He stares for a few seconds, like he's looking at a bug.

"Ewww. Your toes *are* brown! Freak." Tommy turns and runs off after Mrs. Dibben.

I get up. I have to hop on one foot to get my boot and put it back on. I brush some mud and leaves off my sweater, and find my sock, but put it in my pocket. On the ground where I found it, I see the white petals.

When Aiden and I are alone again on the bus ride home, he asks, "How was your field trip?"

I tell him it was fine and tug at the same piece of sticky green tape covering up the hole in the seat in front of us. The day's events swirl in my head. When I got back with my class, everyone was talking about how Natalie had been lying still on the ground and how the ambulance came and took her and her mom away.

It starts to rain. Droplets race down the windows of the bus.

"Is that Tommy kid still bugging you?" Aiden asks.

"No," I say, but I don't look him in the eyes.

Mom is always telling us how being different is a blessing, and how we'll understand when we're older. Right now, I don't believe her. Different means you're different.

The rain comes down hard and crashes against the glass panes and metal roof. I can't see outside anymore. At first it feels like we're in a car wash, but then it's like we're trapped in a long, dark room. It feels weird having one bare foot in my boot, too. Inside my sweater pocket I squeeze my crumpled-up sock. I don't know why I didn't put it back on.

I close my eyes and think of trilliums, but can only see the one that Tommy picked, just leaves and no petals. I wonder how long it will take to flower again, or if it ever will.

When the Good Shines a Little Brighter

ALLY

A few days after my mom flew back to India, my dad was working a weekend shift, so I went to stay with my auntie Audrey, while Aiden went to a friend's. Auntie Audrey wasn't my actual aunt, but we called her that, anyway. On Saturday evening, she made her shrimp curry and rice that we ate at her white kitchen countertop, sitting on heavy stools. Auntie poured me milk into a glass that had a picture of an elephant with the word *Tusker* beneath it.

"Is the curry too spicy for you?" Auntie asked.

"The hotter the better," I said. Just because I was born in Canada, all of my aunts thought I couldn't handle spicy food. When Mom cooked, I'd get her to throw in an extra chili. "Not too many, you kids are already too skinny," she'd say. When Dad ate something hot, beads of sweat rolled down his face.

As I ate, I struggled to remove the shrimp tails with a fork. Auntie had left the shells on the shrimp instead of peeling them off before cooking, like my mom would.

73

"It's okay to use your hands," Auntie said. "Herman used to cook them that way. He thought it gave them more flavour."

I pulled the shells off the shrimp with my hands and stuck my tongue inside to get every last drop of curry. "Can you still braid my hair after we finish?"

"Sure, hon. Did we remember to bring the movie in from the car?"

"Yep, I put it on top of the TV." I had picked *The Lion King* from the rental place. I'd seen it once before in the theatre with my dad and brother. Auntie said she'd only seen the adverts for it. Mom had told me that after Auntie Audrey left India, and before she came to Canada, she had lived in Africa for many years. I was excited to see what she thought of the movie.

AUDREY

It wasn't until 1967 that I finally went on a safari. Herman took me for our honeymoon. He had been on a safari once, before we'd met two years ago, and I'd wanted to go ever since I arrived in Nairobi as a girl and heard the stories of the animals. The elephants especially.

"We'll rent our own Jeep, Audrey. Just you and me," Herman promised.

"You can drive one of those?" I asked.

"Of course. You're lucky you married a jack-of-all-trades."

The wedding had been draining on both of us. We'd held it at Herman's restaurant, which made things easier, but there were still so many guests. My uncle Chester came all the way from South Africa. He was the one who'd first introduced me to Herman, though when Chester said Herman's name it sounded like "Harry-Man."

When I told Herman this the first time we met, I worried he might take it the wrong way, as his head was balding.

But Herman just replied, "When I heard Audrey, I pictured Audrey Hepburn. But you put her to shame."

ALLY

"Was it difficult with your mom gone getting ready for school this week?" Auntie asked, weaving thin bunches of my hair into braids.

I looked back quickly. Her own hair was a mix of black and grey. "Dad helped us," I said, but I didn't tell her that he forgot to do laundry and I had to wear a bathing-suit bottom for underwear one day. He tried his best, but Mom had a way of making Black Forest ham sandwiches taste good, and she put notes in our lunch bags, like *Try your best* or *Make someone smile*. I missed her then.

Auntie gave the top of my head a tap. "Go have a look in the mirror."

I hopped down from the kitchen stool and ran to the giant wooden cabinet in the family room. The handles of the cabinet were elephants' heads, their trunks curled to form loops. On each cabinet door was an oval golden mirror that reflected the room a deep yellow, like a dream. I held up my pigtails and admired them. "Thanks, Auntie," I shouted.

"You're welcome, sweetie. I'll be out in a minute—just going to put the food away and tidy up."

I said, "Okay," but the grandfather clock chimed six o'clock at the same time, and I wasn't sure if she'd heard me. I walked over to the big clock and looked through the clear glass at its swinging heart. My grandpa's heart had stopped working the week before. I never even got to meet him. I'd never met any of my grandparents, only seen black-and-white family photos taken either on a beach or in front of a house with a tiled roof that looked more like a cottage—all smiles from my mom's parents and her and her brothers and sisters. My dad's family pictures were exactly the same, minus the smiles. Aiden and I liked trying to guess which kid was our mom or dad in each picture.

Aiden had gone to India when I wasn't born yet, but now I was eight and still hadn't been. Before Mom flew back a few days ago for my grandpa's funeral, I'd asked her to take me with her. She said this type of visit wasn't for kids. Plus I had school, so it was out of the question.

But I was glad to be with Auntie Audrey instead of the babysitter. She had such interesting things around her living room: skinny wooden shields with faces carved into them, a lamp that looked like it could have a genie inside, and on the coffee table was a game with a board and marbles made of precious stones. Aiden sometimes called Auntie Audrey "Aunt Teek," because she often took us antiquing with her. He never had a good time, but I loved it. We went to all kinds of places: garage sales, trading posts, and small shops with bells above the doors that jingled when you walked in or out.

"Searching high and low for nothing in particular," Auntie would say. Even though everything we found in the stores was old, it was all new to me. There were dolls, drawings, chairs, sewing machines, fancy knives and forks, and old tools I couldn't recognize. Last time, Auntie and I bought a wooden end table, which sat in the corner of the living room with a circular top and bottom, and a woman carved into the wood between.

As we were leaving for our trip, Herman surprised me with a bouquet of roses on the front seat of the car. The roses were yellow with red tips and looked like little flames. I gave him a sloppy kiss before he started the car. He had booked a safari guide for five o'clock that evening, and we'd eaten an early lunch of mutton curry and chapatis leftover from the wedding. I had packed some in a metal tiffin to take with us, along with a canteen of water and two bottles of Coca-Cola.

The drive to the Masai Mara was long, the road spotted with stray rocks and potholes. Herman weaved to avoid them without slowing down for all but the most treacherous. I'd moved the roses to the back seat, and with the windows open they fluttered in the breeze. As we motored along, I took slow sips of Coca-Cola with my other arm out the window, my hand floating and bouncing on the air rushing by. When it started to rain, I kept my arm outside, enjoying the cool, tingling drops; in the short rain season, the clouds changed their minds quickly, and often.

A couple of hours into the drive, Herman pointed to something on the road in the distance. "What's that up there?"

I squinted. "Looks like cows."

We got closer and slowed down, eventually stopping for a herd crossing the road. The cows were brown, white, or black, or a mix of those colours. A cloud of red dust rose around them. The sounds of their shuffling, mooing, and bells blended into one droning noise.

Herman pointed again. "Look—Masai warriors."

The men walking amongst the cows wore red checkered cloth and beads around their heads and necks. They were tall and skinny, just like the long sticks they used to herd the cows and protect them from becoming prey.

My eyes were drawn to a pond off the road where a few Masai women were collecting water in clay pots. One woman placed a rolled cloth on her head. She bent down, lifted the heavy pot, and settled it on top of the roll. For the first few steps, she held the pot with one hand for balance, but then she let go as she found her stride. The women were warriors, too.

ALLY

While Auntie did the dishes, I went upstairs to use the bathroom. The soap smelled like peaches. Down the hall from the bathroom were her kids' old bedrooms. The beds were made and the kids' framed degrees hung on the walls. They were adults now, and lived in different cities. I wondered how Auntie lived in such a big house by herself.

I came back downstairs and into the family room. Between the couch and the fireplace was the end table we'd bought last time we went antiquing. The woman carved into the table stood tall, with long legs, and arms that held the tabletop over her head. Auntie had told me what the name for the woman in the table was, but I couldn't remember.

I ran my hands along the smooth wood but took a few steps back when I saw the small golden urn on top of the fireplace mantel. The ashes of Auntie's husband were in there. He'd died when I was younger. The one thing I remembered about him was how he always carried hard candy in his pocket.

Auntie's voice startled me. "All set for the movie?"

"Yep," I said, and turned away from the urn.

I was so entranced by the women that when the cows finally cleared the road, I wanted to go talk to them instead of leaving. But Herman was worried about our scheduled safari and that we were already late. Through the back window, I watched the women recede. As we drove, the road got bumpier and the grass grew greener; the hills rose and fell from the earth like soft waves in the sea.

"We'll have to quickly drop off our stuff at the lodge." With one hand on the wheel, Herman fiddled with the dial on the binoculars hanging around his neck. "Then we can head back out to see if we can catch some of the action."

"Okay. I'll have to go pee, though." I held up my empty Coca-Cola bottle.

Herman gazed out into the savannah. "Look at all of those trucks."

Five or six ivory-coloured vehicles like our own were clustered just off the roadside. "What do you think they're looking at?"

"I don't know, but we should go check it out."

"I thought we were going to drop our stuff off first."

"Whatever they're looking at may be gone by then." Herman pressed the brakes and steered off the road, toward the other trucks.

As we drew closer to the other safari trucks filled with tourists, we saw a pair of lions lying on the grass.

I rolled up my window. "We're so close! They're not going to try to attack us?"

"As long as we stay in the vehicle, they see us as some big dumb animal they can't eat and who isn't trying to eat them."

"You're sure?"

"Positive." Herman waved to the drivers and passengers in

the other trucks nearby. He handed me the binoculars, but I didn't need them. We were that close.

The lioness was lying on her belly, her paws stretched in front of her. The male lion was standing; he had a full, chestnut-coloured mane and stared off into the distance. The lion's stance suggested it was hungry, but not for food.

I turned to Herman, excited, and said, "I think they're going to mate."

The male swaggered up behind the female and lay on top of her. I couldn't help but laugh; Herman joined me.

The male licked and bit the lioness's neck. She glanced back and showed her fangs but didn't move away. The male's body pumped for less than thirty seconds before stopping.

"That was quick," I said.

"Not at all like *your* lion," Herman said, with a peck on my neck.

The lioness rolled on her side. The male stood and circled her once, before falling sideways with his body first, then letting his head drop to the ground.

ALLY

"Simba!" Auntie said. We were watching the movie from the carpet instead of the couch. "That's the actual word for lion in Swahili."

"What's Swahili?" I asked.

"It's the language they speak in Kenya, and a few other countries."

All of the animals in the movie were singing. "How long ago did you live there?"

"We came to Canada in seventy-eight, so almost twenty years. Gosh, that seems like a long time." She shook her head

80

slowly. "Now, don't ask me how long ago I moved from Goa—I wouldn't be able to tell you."

While Simba sang about how he couldn't wait to be king, my eyes were drawn to the end table with the woman.

"Auntie, what is that lady holding the table called?"

"It's a caryatid figure."

"But what does it mean?"

"It's a name for a woman carved into a supporting structure. You see them as stone pillars on old buildings. They remind me of the women of our culture. Under great stress, they remain strong. You know, we come from long lines of strong women, and you inherited that strength."

I looked at the table again. "I think my arms would get tired after a while."

Auntie laughed; she had a loud laugh that made me laugh along. "It's in you," she said, "don't worry."

I looked around the room—it was like everything here had a story. I avoided looking at the urn and asked, "Which antique is your favourite?"

"That one's very special because we both picked it out, but I don't think I've got a favourite. There's something about each piece I love. They hold on to a time and place that doesn't exist anymore. And help you remember the way things used to be."

"Did you like antiques when you were my age?"

"How old are you now?"

"Eight."

"Eight already! Both you and your brother look so much younger than your age, just like your mother and father."

"Is that another thing I inherited?"

"Yes, indeed. I swear, time touches your family's faces more gently than others'. Now, when I was your age, regretfully, I didn't like antiques. Our house in Goa was full of them, too, and we didn't even know it. We took all those old things for granted, and played with them and broke them. There were so many things in Africa that would be antiques now, too, but we couldn't take any of them with us. We had to leave it all behind when we came here."

AUDREY

Herman and I were watching the lions laze around when, one by one, all the other drivers got on their radios, started their engines, and began to drive back to the road.

"They must have heard of something else," Herman said. "We should get going."

"Yes, and I still have to pee, Herman."

"Oh yes, sorry! Let's go."

Less than a mile later, I noticed something on the horizon beyond the silhouette of a few acacia trees. I looked through the binoculars. "Elephants!"

"Where?" Herman asked.

"Your side. Let's go, Herman."

"I thought you had to pee?"

"I can hold it for elephants."

"But we'll miss our safari."

"This *is* a safari." I put my hand on Herman's hand that held the steering wheel. "Let's quickly see them and then head back."

Again, we turned off the road, but this time had to go farther to get close enough to see the animals.

The farther we drove, the damper and more exposed the grass became, as if we were following the path that the elephants had stamped down.

We approached the acacias, the trees revealing individual thorns, leaves, and branches, and one of the bigger elephants trumpeted a warning to let us know we'd come close enough. Herman stopped the Jeep.

We'd been closer with the lions, but through the binoculars I could clearly see a family of ten elephants, including a baby. "So cute!" I said. The calf's walk was clumsy amongst the giants all around, but it was never knocked over.

The sun was setting behind us, casting the savannah in an amber glow. A glow I felt as well. The animals were engrossing: lumbering steps and quick twists of the tail, grand flapping ears and swinging trunks that gently probed. Like a dance.

Herman put his hand on my shoulder and said, "We should get going."

I realized the sun had set and light was fading. "Yes, let's go," I said. "I'm glad we came."

Herman turned the Jeep around in the direction of the road. We both saw the muddy depression in the grass too late. Our front tires made it through okay, but the back tires sank into the thick mud. We tilted forward in our seats as the Jeep lurched to a stop.

Herman stepped on the gas. The wheels spun and sent mud flying behind us. He tried going in reverse, also without luck.

"Hakuna matata," he said. "Let me get out and give it a push."

"You're going outside?"

"Just right here."

I looked around to see if there was any wildlife in sight; the elephants were once again dots on the horizon, and it felt like they were abandoning us.

"When I tell you, press the gas to the floor."

"Be careful."

I moved into the driver's seat. On the count of three, we tried four times to push, before realizing we were royally stuck.

Herman returned to the Jeep. "Someone will be by."

"All the way out here?" I looked out the window. The acacias now looked menacing and the tall, wavering grass looked like anything could come crawling out of it. "Herman?"

"Yes."

"I have to pee."

ALLY

When Simba was lured into the canyon, both Auntie and I fell silent. After the wildebeest had stampeded, and the cloud of dust had cleared away from his father, I thought again of my grandpa, and Mom going to see him.

"Did you know my grandpa?" I asked Auntie.

"I met him when I was younger, but we moved soon after. I heard he was a nice man, though."

"How come he died?"

Auntie took a deep breath. "You know he had troubles with his heart."

"I know, but why did he die before I met him?"

"That's a very hard question to answer, honey." She let the breath out in a long, slow exhale. "Every day I ask myself why my Herman had to die, and I don't think there's an answer that makes sense. Every morning I come downstairs and touch that urn on the mantel." She raised a single finger, as if saying hello. "Herman wanted his ashes spread across the plains where we went for our honeymoon. But I haven't been able to move the urn from that spot since the day I brought it home. Before Herman was diagnosed, we had always talked about going back to visit, but never made the trip in time."

Auntie rubbed her eye. I couldn't tell if she was hiding a tear, and I wondered if she needed a hug. But she just got up, her knees cracking. "How about some ice cream, Ally? Think you can squeeze it in?"

She went to the kitchen and I looked at the urn on the mantel again. I didn't turn away this time. I went closer, reached up, and touched the urn lightly with my finger. It was cool and smooth. I wasn't scared. I went to go give Auntie a hug, but when I peeked around the kitchen corner, she was sitting on the stool with her face in her hands.

AUDREY

My knees cracked as I squatted just outside the open door of the Jeep. I'd told Herman not to look while I went, but also to watch out for predators in the growing dark.

Just as I was finishing, I spotted something small moving in the distance. I pulled my shorts back up in a hurry, dove back into the Jeep, and shut the door. "What is that there?"

Herman squinted through the binoculars. "Just a Thomson's gazelle. Not going eat you."

I took the binoculars and saw the tiny deerlike animal with a tail that spun like a propeller. As it ran away, I took a few deep breaths to steady myself.

"I should just walk back to the road and get help," Herman said.

"You'll do no such thing." I buttoned up my shorts. "We need to remain calm. Now, if we're relatively safe in the car, then we are going to stay here."

"The whole night?"

"We should have enough water, and we still have that mutton curry. Thank goodness we packed it."

Herman scratched the top of his head. "I suppose you're right."

We listened as the chorus of nocturnal insects began to grow louder, as if signalling an uneasy awakening around us.

ALLY

I didn't think Auntie wanted me to know she was crying, so I didn't go give her a hug. After a couple of minutes I called out from the family room, "You're going to miss the good part, Auntie," hoping it would help cheer her up.

She came back with two bowls and handed me one. She had sprinkled nutmeg on top of the vanilla ice cream. I hadn't had it like that before and it tasted great, but I still felt bad for her.

"Hakuna matata," she sang, along with the movie.

"No worries. I know that one," I said.

"Yes, no problem. I haven't heard that in years. And Pumbaa's name means 'silly.' This movie brings back so many memories." Auntie stared at the TV screen for a minute before continuing. "I'll always cherish my time in Kenya. All our children were born there. Herman started our first restaurant there, too. Such a busy and stressful time it was. We had to work very, very hard, but it all seemed so worthwhile." A spoonful of ice cream hovered over and dripped into her bowl. "If I could only go back—it was just...golden."

It felt like she actually did go there. She sat still, staring at the TV screen, but wasn't watching the movie. For a moment it seemed like I was alone in the house, but she came back a few seconds later, sliding the spoon back into her bowl.

"I suppose everyone has a time in their life they'd like to return to, where they forget the bad and the good shines a little brighter."

The stars were out in the sky when Herman and I shared the small meal from the metal tiffin. With our hands, we tore chapatis and pinched up mutton and sauce.

Herman licked his fingers as he finished the last bite. "We're lucky the lions haven't tasted my mutton curry. We'd be in big trouble if so."

"You're a better cook than you are a driver, mister jack-of-all-trades."

Herman kissed me on the cheek and pulled two hard caramel candies out of his pocket. "Dessert."

I smiled, running my fingers across the top of his smooth, bald head. "My Harry-Man."

I took his bottom lip in between mine, but we were interrupted by an elephant trumpeting in the distance. We looked out the windows and listened. Nothing. And then Harry was kissing me again, and we forgot all that was outside. The windows of the Jeep fogged up until we couldn't see the stars.

ALLY

Auntie and I clinked our spoons around the inside of our ice cream bowls for the last melted drops.

"Ally, did I tell you what happened to Herman and me on our honeymoon safari?"

I shook my head.

"Our Jeep got stuck in the mud and we ended up spending the whole night out in the wild."

"What did you do all night?"

Auntie had a smile on her face. "Oh, you know. *Talked.*"

"How did you get out?"

"In the morning another truck came by and used a winch to pull us free."

"Do you think you'll ever go back?" I asked.

Auntie put her bowl down beside her. "I'm not sure. Ally, I think you ask more questions than all of my kids combined."

I was glad to hear her laugh again. "Mom said you should never stop asking questions," I said. "Because then God will think that you've gotten all of your answers."

"Your mother is a very smart lady. I think Herman would want me asking more questions, too."

In the morning, I put my shoes on in the foyer to get ready for my dad, who was on his way to pick me up. I thanked Auntie for the blueberry oatmeal breakfast and for taking care of me. She said it was her pleasure.

After I finished tying my laces, I stood up and noticed something different in the family room. The urn of Auntie's husband wasn't on the mantel. It was on the end table.

Auntie caught me staring, and said, "One step closer to Africa. Think she's strong enough?"

I looked from the woman under the table to my aunt standing over me, and knew she was.

Two Islands

The ferry's engine hummed, and you could taste the salt in the breeze. Thomas and Emma sat on hard plastic chairs with their luggage by their feet. They had left Port Blair a few hours earlier, but the boat ride on the Andaman Sea had not felt long until that stocky man, also from the UK, came over to chat with them.

"So, which island are you two going to?" asked the man. "Let me guess—Havelock?"

"Seems to be the consensus on board," Emma said.

"Some of the most beautiful, most secluded beaches in India—so says Lonely Planet. Best of the Andaman Islands, I'm sure." The man wore a beige, wide-brimmed hat, the kind you might wear on a desert safari. His collared shirt matched his hat, and dark chest hair sprouted above the last fastened button.

"Well, beauty is a matter of taste. Don't you think?" Thomas said.

The man's puzzled look vanished when the ferry's engine stalled and restarted with a judder, sending him wobbling around the deck. "Bloody hell," he said, grabbing the railing. "I'll be making a complaint when I get back to Port Blair. I guarantee India wasn't run this way when it was under the British Empire."

Thomas turned to Emma, who was holding her stomach and looking sick. He passed her his water bottle and said to the man, "I think most Indian people would disagree with you. And we're actually going to Neil Island."

"Are you daft, man?" He pulled out his guidebook and opened it to a bookmarked and highlighted page. "Listen to what it says about Havelock: 'White sand, dazzling sunsets, and still untouched by tourists.' Here, look at that picture! There's your proof."

Thomas glanced at the photo. The beach was as picturesque as all the beaches in this part of the world. In actual fact, he and Emma hadn't decided which island they were going to, but however large Havelock Island was, it wouldn't be large enough if they had to share it with the man in the safari hat.

Emma took another sip of water and said, "It looks nice."

The man grinned smugly.

"Look, I don't care what the guidebook says," Thomas argued. "If this is the *only* ferry from Port Blair going to the two islands, and *everyone else* is getting off at one island, then doesn't it stand to reason that the other one will have fewer tourists?"

He turned away and stared at the horizon, ignoring Emma's placating hand on his thigh all the way into port at Havelock Island.

Thomas and Emma continued to sit there while all the other passengers rolled their luggage down the ramp and onto the dock. Emma spun her engagement ring around her finger as she waited; the gold band had a dolphin jumping over a small diamond. Thomas had proposed in December, right after finishing his masters in sociology. She'd said she loved the ring, dolphins were her favourite, but joked that when he started teaching full-time, maybe the dolphin could jump over something bigger.

Thomas had been led to believe the ring was mostly for her friends and family, so he was surprised when she'd said that.

Thomas had been offered a place in the doctoral program starting in the fall, but he wasn't certain if he'd accept. After six years of higher education he was ready for a break. So they'd come to India, their first real vacation together. Emma had been drawn to the colourful clothing and jewellery in the pictures she'd seen. She'd studied textiles and worked in fashion. Thomas had wanted to go to India ever since he was a boy and his uncle returned with a carved stone chess set for him, as well as stories of Hindu gods, train rides, festivals, and wandering cows.

There was so much Thomas had wanted to see in India, but Emma could only get three weeks off work, so they'd agreed that he'd leave a few weeks early. Their original plan was to meet in Goa for a beach vacation, and then head to Agra to see the Taj Mahal before flying back to England. But their Goa plans were cut short, and now they were in the Andamans.

There was a binocular contraption for tourists welded to one section of the ferry's rail. Thomas leaned in and pointed it at the debarking passengers. He saw the safari hat man by the road bickering with a rickshaw driver. All around him, young women with gold ear and nose rings tempted the tourists with a rainbow of fruit on banana-leaf plates. Thomas wanted to get off the ferry and buy some sliced pineapple, but the crew was readying things to set off again.

As their boat began to putter away, Thomas watched his fellow countryman finally seat himself in the rickshaw. The young driver pushed down on the pedals with all his weight, but had what looked to be a wide grin on his face; he must have negotiated a good price. It reminded Thomas of the advice he'd gotten from a nice woman from Canada named Clara, who he'd met on the long train journey from Mumbai to Goa.

Clara had been sitting opposite him, and the moment the

train groaned into motion, a man squeezed into the berth beside Thomas and began to pick his nose. He used his long index finger to dig through each nasal cavity, then rubbed the nostril treasures between his thumb and finger until they dropped to the train floor. A thorough cleaning. Thomas tried not to stare, and opened his *Condensed History of India*, a surprisingly thick book, and his train-ticket bookmark fell out. It said *Bombay*, even though they'd recently changed the name to Mumbai, and as he picked it up, Thomas noticed Clara holding back a smile.

The man picking his nose finally stopped. Thomas had based his master's thesis on the idea that social deviance and acceptability are culturally specific. So maybe in India this sort of thing was okay.

Yet when the man exited the berth, Clara said to Thomas, "Takes some getting used to, doesn't it?"

"Hard not to notice. Sorry, it's my first trip to India."

"I see you're reading up."

"Just learning all the terrible things my country did to India."

"That's more than I can say for most tourists. And what do you think of my country so far?" Clara had long black hair and wore a thin gold necklace that held a small cross. Thomas had a necklace like hers that his parents had given him when he was a kid, though it sat in a small box in the bottom drawer of his dresser back home.

"I love it. So far it's been brilliant." Thomas told Clara how he had started in Delhi, travelled through Rajasthan, and then down to Mumbai. And was now headed to Goa to meet his fiancée.

"I'm from Goa," Clara continued, "but I live in Canada now with my husband and children." She pulled out a photo from her handbag. "That's Aiden, such a smart boy he is, first in his class, but he always seems to get himself into trouble. And that's

Ally, sweetest little girl you'll ever meet, but try to get her to concentrate on something for more than a few minutes, and she'll be running up the walls."

From his wallet, Thomas took out a picture of him and Emma with their faces smooshed together. He'd held the camera as high and as far as his arm would allow, but you could still tell he'd taken the photo, and not someone else.

"Lovely," Clara remarked.

Conversation came easily between them, flowing alongside the landscape that passed out the train window: rice paddies and palms, green hills, blue lakes, beige villages.

Thomas was curious why she touched the cross around her neck from time to time, and eventually he felt comfortable enough to ask.

"My trip is one of bereavement, for my father." But when Thomas offered his condolences, she seemed almost dismissive: "This is life. Beginnings, endings."

They talked until it was late, then folded their respective sleeper beds down from the wall and retired to the clacking and steady chug of the train over the tracks. In the morning, they resumed their conversation.

"So, what do you and Emma have planned for Goa?"

"Probably just lying on the beach," Thomas said with an embarrassed laugh, adding, "Emma hasn't travelled much outside the UK. I'm a bit nervous, actually."

"Baptism by fire," Clara joked. She then suggested a good place to take Emma might be the pavilion with the statue of Dona Paula. Goa's Romeo and Juliet.

As they approached their destination, they exchanged addresses, Clara including where she'd be staying in Goa, just in case he and Emma got tired of the beach. *Colvale, Khursa Vaddo,* she'd written, but instead of a house number it only said *near St. Mary's school, opposite the late Father Constantine's nephew's home.*

"All the addresses there are like that," she clarified. "Just ask anyone and they'll point you in the right direction."

Clara's stop was one earlier than Thomas's, and as the train slowed, she gave him some last-minute advice on the price of a rickshaw ride to the airport. "Never accept the first price. Whatever they offer, react like they've just asked for a fortune."

She waved goodbye, and Thomas continued his journey. He was looking forward to greeting Emma, and hoped she'd had a wonderful chance meeting like he'd just had.

"How are you feeling?" Thomas asked Emma. They'd returned to their seats on the ship's deck, though they were now the only ones aboard.

"My stomach's still not right," she said. "Maybe we should have gotten off." But it was too late; the island was receding as the ferry chugged through the ocean.

"I promise I won't make you eat any more pakoras with your pizza and banana fritters," Thomas joked.

"Ugh, please don't remind me." Emma recoiled. "You weren't the one with your arse on the toilet and face in the rubbish bin for three days."

"Do I at least get credit for finding you ginger ale? It was an epic search."

Emma shook her head.

"I still think it wouldn't have been as bad if you'd agreed to see a doctor," Thomas said. "Then we could have gone to another hotel or beach in Goa, instead of the other end of India."

"You know I don't trust the medication. And that place just reminded me of being sick." Emma shuddered and turned away from him.

Thomas put his arm around her shoulders and rubbed her back. "You're right. I guess it doesn't make a difference if we get our beach time here instead."

But as he stared at the skyline, he wished he could have stayed in Goa longer. He had hoped to take Emma to visit Clara's village, but it was too far from their hotel. Dona Paula, the site Clara had told him about, was close by and he went on his own the day before they left. Emma was feeling a bit better but didn't want to come, and seeing all the couples there made Thomas wish she had, but he was glad he got to see at least one thing in Goa.

Another island began to take shape on the horizon, and Emma said, "There it is. I hope this place is better."

Thomas eyed the island and promised, "It will be."

"Namaste," the hotel's proprietor greeted them at the reception desk. The man's forehead shone, his hair in retreat. A few remaining strands danced in the breeze from a small fan pointed directly at his face.

"Namaste, bhaiya." Thomas had been practising.

"Hello there, we need a room with air-con," said Emma.

"Of course, of course. You two will be very pleased here," the man said.

Thomas picked up a business card from the desk. The "o" in *Sunrise Hotel* was a cartoon sun with a smile, and the name *Mr. Lakhani* was printed in bold underneath.

"How is the sunrise here?" Thomas asked.

"The best," the proprietor said, with a circular head bob. "You must see it to know."

"How much for a room?"

"Three hundred rupees a night."

"Three hundred! That's outrageous." Thomas tried to use Clara's technique. "I'll give you one hundred."

"Oh, no no no. It cannot be done, I would go out of business if I gave you such a price. The least I can give you is two hundred and seventy-five rupees."

"How about two hundred?" The ferry crew said the next closest accommodation was a ten-minute walk from where they were dropped off. Thomas was sure Emma wouldn't want to walk it.

"Two-fifty, then. Yes?"

Thomas nodded, with pride. Emma rolled her eyes.

"Very good. It is a most special time you have come now; you have the whole hotel to yourselves." Mr. Lakhani opened a wide logbook. "Passports?"

They handed him their passports and he neatly recorded the details in the ledger. Thomas glanced at the "Nationality" column. The last guests were Indian citizens and they'd checked out a few days ago.

"Visa expires October 2000?" said Mr. Lakhani. "I've never seen a five-year visa to India before. How did you get this?"

"I just applied. It wasn't much more than a one-year visa, so I figured I might as well."

"Planning on coming back, I think. How long will you be staying this trip?"

"We're not quite sure, maybe just over a week," Thomas said.

"Let's not commit for so long, Thomas," Emma said.

"Why not?"

Mr. Lakhani interjected, "I'm sorry, sir and madam, but the maximum time allowed for foreigners to stay is four days."

"But you just said we're the only ones here," Thomas said.

"These are the hotel rules. If you like, you can take the ferry back to Port Blair, get a new stamp, then come back and stay another four days." He handed back their passports.

"That makes no sense."

"Tom, let's just take it day by day." Emma handed over the 250 rupees and took the key in return.

A woman in a pink sari stepped into the reception room.

Atop her head, a woven basket seemed to balance by the radiance of her smile alone.

"This is Jasmine." Mr. Lakhani didn't look up from counting his money. "Should you need anything at all, just let her know."

"Nice to meet you," Emma said, as she picked up her bags. Jasmine gave a slight bow, careful not to topple the basket. Thomas felt struck when his eyes met Jasmine's, as if they were alone in the room; not until Emma started to walk toward their room did he turn away. He picked up his bag and joined Emma.

Once out of range of the desk, Emma said, "Tom, that man is clearly just trying to get us to pay more with that whole thing about only being able to stay four days."

"You think so?" Thomas still felt a bit dazed.

"Isn't that what everyone does in this country? It's all about money. We should try to bribe him and see."

Room 101 was small but clean. A tall mirror sat on a table that held two sealed rolls of toilet paper, two small bars of soap wrapped in paper, and two bottles of spring water. Thomas and Emma tossed their bags on the bleached white sheets of the double bed. Thomas was relieved when he saw the Western-style toilet. He had forgotten to ask at the desk and didn't know what they would have done if there wasn't one; Emma refused to squat. Luckily her stomach had settled enough for them to go to the beach.

They changed into their bathing suits, locked up, and followed the sound of the waves along an old wooden-plank path. Warm white sand filled the spaces between their toes, and the sun was bright and strong. Halfway down the empty beach they stopped to spread their towels, a wall of palm trees over their shoulders and the turquoise water beyond their feet. Thomas thought back to that annoying man on the ferry—if it wasn't for him, they wouldn't even be on this island, let alone this beach.

"This is stunning!" Emma said.

Relieved, Thomas leaned over and gave her a quick kiss. "A beautiful beach, all to ourselves."

"Well, almost to ourselves." Emma squinted, then pointed. "Look, there's someone."

A man in cut-off jean shorts and a linen shirt was walking in their direction along the shore. As he got closer, Thomas could tell he wasn't Indian, but couldn't quite place him. The tanned skin and sunglasses didn't help. On top of his head was a large pair of earmuff headphones connected to a portable CD player in his hand. He walked along the water's edge so that the waves just barely wet his bare feet, and continued right past them, down the beach.

"Huh, he didn't even notice us," said Emma.

"Yeah. Off in his own world, I guess."

"Oh well. *I* am going for a swim."

Thomas watched her walk to the water like she was on a runway, wade in to her waist, then dive under. She re-emerged two body lengths away, chestnut hair slicked back.

Meanwhile, the man with the headphones had become nothing more than a dark speck down the beach.

"Are you going to join me?" Emma called from the water.

Thomas got up and splashed his way toward her until their bodies met. She put her arms on his shoulders, hands clasped behind his neck. His hands cupped her buttocks underwater. Their lips wet with salt water, they kissed.

But then Emma pulled away with a panicked look. She took her arms off his shoulders and held her hand in front of her.

"Oh my god. Thomas. My ring, I've lost my ring!"

"Where? Just now?"

"I don't know, I think so. It must've come off in the water."

They separated and began to look around. The shallow water was perfectly translucent, yet they saw nothing. The sun's light dived in and danced underwater, but it failed to give glitter to the ring.

"There's so much sand."

"Emma, we'll find it."

"You should have reminded me to take it off."

"How would I think to do that? Let's just keep looking."

They searched for ten minutes before Emma said, "This is pointless. I'm going to check the room."

Thomas stayed in the sea looking, but the sun was making him thirsty and he wished he had brought those water bottles from their room. After a while, Jasmine appeared with two football-sized coconuts with straws poking out. They met at his towel, and she handed him one of the coconuts.

"Dhanyavad. Thank you." Thomas took a long sip through the straw and the sweet water cooled his throat.

"Your lady friend?" Jasmine held up the other coconut. She had a tiny red bindi on her forehead that he hadn't noticed the first time he'd seen her.

"Oh, she went back to the room. She lost her ring in the sea."

"Oh no. I'm sorry. I look."

"No, no. You don't have to do that. It's okay. Thank you, though."

"I pray you find. No tell Mr. Lahkani. Many people search, and keep."

"That's very kind of you. Thank you."

Jasmine left to deliver the other drink to Emma. A vanilla fragrance lingered in the air as she walked away.

Thomas woke up early the next day to a symphony of birds. Emma was still asleep, so he closed the door quietly and made his way to the beach to search for the ring. It would be expensive to have to buy another one. He arrived in those few minutes when it was still light out but the sun hadn't yet shown its face.

When he saw Jasmine bathing in the water, he froze. Her wet hair hung below her shoulders. Fully covered in a soaked orange sarong, she lathered herself with graceful strokes and sent controlled splashes from a small plastic bucket over each part of her body. It was beautiful. Just as the thought came to Thomas that he shouldn't be watching her, she noticed him. She revealed that irresistible smile again and waved at him without a pinch of shame. Thomas managed to wave back before he fled to his room.

He lay next to Emma and tried to go back to sleep, but he couldn't get the image of Jasmine in the water out of his mind.

He got out of bed to take a shower. As the steam rose around him, he thought back to something Clara had said to him about India on the train. They had just bought samosas and chai. Clara took a small bite from her samosa and blew inside to cool it.

"Above all, India is a land that evokes emotion," she told him. "We are surrounded by people here, many of them poor, yet rich in heart. And so many hearts close together have a way of bringing forth emotions like nothing else. Eventually, people's true natures are revealed."

Thomas took a sip of his chai.

"It's a well-known fact that there are more gods than people here," she continued. "But the emotions experienced on any one day far exceed the number of gods."

In the shower, Thomas was torn from his thoughts when the water ran cold and he had to jump out of its path.

Emma was waking up as he came back into the bedroom.

"Did you catch the sunrise?" she asked.

"No, no. I missed it," he mumbled, and watched her walk sleepily into the loo. "I think the hot water is broken."

"You used it all up?"

"It just went cold. I wasn't in there long."

The door shut, and Thomas heard a loud groan from inside the bathroom.

Thomas was thinking about the ring during their omelette brunch, and again when he and Emma were back on their towels on the beach. Emma put on sunscreen and handed him the bottle. He'd hoped to get some more colour to his skin, so he put the sunscreen on the towel next to his *Condensed History of India*.

Emma flipped through the glossy pages of a few fashion magazines she'd brought from home, including the one she edited.

"I'm gonna go have another look for your ring." Thomas stood up. "Care to join me?"

Emma shielded her eyes from the sun and held her page with an index finger. "I'm over it, hon."

"Don't get *emotional* or anything. I'd think you'd be a little bit more upset about losing your engagement ring."

"What do you want me to do, Tom? There's no way we'll find it in all that sand and water." She let out a long breath. "I'm going to see if the phone is working so I can call home."

Thomas stood, his hands on his hips, and watched her walk away, then turned to the sea. He was about to head back when he saw the man with headphones walking along the shore, just like yesterday. As he passed right by again, Thomas chased the man and called out to him from behind. He didn't respond, so Thomas swung around in front of him. The man looked up and gave Thomas a surprised frown that changed to a grin.

He took off his headphones. "Hola."

"Sorry to surprise you like that," Thomas said.

"No problem. Was just listening to some music." He held up the CD player, then shook Thomas's hand and said his name was José.

"What brings you to the Andamans?" Thomas asked.

José raised both hands and looked around. "This, my friend. You as well?"

"It's gorgeous. Don't get weather like this in England. I just arrived yesterday with my fiancée. Though unfortunately she already lost her engagement ring in the water."

"Oh no, that's terrible. She must be heartbroken."

Thomas agreed.

José said he would keep his eyes open, and added, "If you two need cheering up, you should come to the other side of the island. I am playing the club there on Saturday night."

"You're a DJ?"

"Just for the next two weeks. Spain is home. Ibiza. I just finished recording and this was supposed to be a vacation. But I can't get far from music. It is my life. And you, Thomas?"

"Actually, I did a bit of DJing myself back in day." Thomas had only ever messed around with a friend's deck but he wanted to impress José.

"That is perfect! My friend, can you do me a favour?"

"What kind of favour?"

"I've got a problem on this island, too. Four days I've walked these beaches trying to decide between two of my tracks. Could you listen and tell me which one you like better?"

Thomas agreed, and José gave him the headphones; they covered his ears wholly. On the first track, a man sang, *Hey oh oh*, before a playful flute and an easy beat came in. The song kept getting faster and adding layers—a woman's *mmm*, a few Spanish words—and Thomas bobbed his head with his eyes closed while the waves died softly at his feet. He enjoyed the second song, too, but it had more of an ambient feel.

Thomas gave the headphones back. "You made these?"

"Yes, yes, I made them. But which one do you prefer?"

"If I had to pick one, it would be the first. I don't know, it just has this...energy."

"Yes! Gracias, my friend." He grabbed Thomas's hand and pulled him in for a hug. "I think I was leaning toward that one but needed someone to say it. That one will go on the album."

"What album?"

"My album. I needed to choose the final track, and now I have my answer."

Before they parted, Thomas promised he'd bring Emma to José's club. José walked away with headphones in hand, his pace a little quicker, humming the chosen song. Thomas felt suddenly motivated to keep searching for Emma's ring.

Back at his towel he was greeted once again by Jasmine carrying two coconuts. She handed him one and asked about Emma. Thomas told her that his fiancée had gone to make a call, but Jasmine didn't understand, so he made a phone gesture with his hand against his head.

"Sorry, my English no good," Jasmine said.

"No. Your English is fantastic. Much better than my Hindi. Where did you learn?"

"From hotel guests. They no teach me, I listen and learn. I no read, no write."

"That's still amazing you picked it up from just listening to guests."

"Yes, one day, when I learn read, write, I start school on island. Bring all the kids."

"That's a very admirable goal. You should ask Mr. Lakhani to teach you to read. He's not your father, is he?"

"No. Mr. Lakhani boss. My father fisherman. Very good fisherman. You like to go fish?"

"I'd love to do some fishing. He'd take me? Only if it's no trouble."

"No trouble, he take you tomorrow. After breakfast. And Miss Emma?"

"I'll ask her."

"She is your wife? Yes?"

"No, we aren't married. How about you, Jasmine?"

"I am no married."

They both turned to see Mr. Lakhani summoning Jasmine from the edge of the wood path, calling out that other guests had arrived.

Thomas had a tingly feeling as Jasmine walked away between the coconut trees and disappeared from his view.

The way the coconut tree leaves swayed in the wind reminded Thomas of the view from Dona Paula, in Goa. After climbing the steps of the large pavilion, he had looked back at the shore, and it was as if the wind were meeting the tree's branches with short waves to match the water below. Thomas took a picture of the coconut trees stretched across the sand, then moved higher up the steps to see the statue of the lovers who had thrown themselves off the black-rock cliff. On the train, Clara had told him she had come here not long before getting married. She'd known the man who would become her husband since they were children, but another man was trying hard for her love. Thomas remembered her saying, "Seeing those statues, I asked myself, 'Who would you want holding your hand if you were jumping off a cliff?' Then it became easy."

Thomas tried to imagine Emma and him jumping off a cliff together—but why would they need to?

Thomas drank his Kingfisher beer in the dining area, waiting for Emma to join him for dinner. The hot water had been fixed, so she was taking a shower.

The new guests were an Indian family accompanied by two security guards, and they were finishing up their meal two tables over from Thomas. The uniformed guards were positioned by the doorway. After the woman and two children finished eating, they left the table, but the man stayed behind with his beer.

When Thomas made eye contact, the man pushed out the chair next to him and said, "Care to join me?" He wore thin wire-frame glasses and, despite the heat, a navy blazer.

Thomas walked over and they introduced themselves. The man rolled the "r" when saying Rishi, and Thomas cautiously eyed the security guards as he repeated it.

Rishi asked where Thomas was from, then told him about his trip to London. Thomas guessed he might own some kind of business and was too curious about the guards not to ask.

"Just a formality. You see, I'm the minister of tourism." He took a sip of beer, then continued. "I'd be interested to hear what brought you to Neil Island. You don't see many tourists here."

"Actually, we almost went to Havelock Island."

"Oh, it's a good thing you didn't!" Rishi let out an odd laugh more like a child's giggle than the practised chuckle of a politician. "I was told the bugs came early this year on Havelock Island."

"Well, looks like I made the right choice."

"Always follow to your instincts. That is what has got me this far." He pushed his eyeglasses up on his nose. "So, you are enjoying my country so far?"

"I love it."

"Very good. Is there anything you can suggest? It's not often I get to speak with visitors."

"My only complaint is that we're not allowed to stay longer." Rishi gave Thomas a puzzled look, so he continued. "We were told that foreigners are only allowed to stay for four days and then have to go back to Port Blair if they want to return."

"Bhaiya," Rishi called out to the next room.

Mr. Lakhani came rushing over. "Yes, sir, what can I do for you?"

"Why is my friend Thomas only allowed to stay for four days?"

"Yes, that is the rule for foreigners."

"Well, we're going to change that, yes? They should be allowed to stay as long as they like."

"Yes, sir, not a problem. They can stay as long as they like." How quickly Mr. Lakhani's disposition changed from superior to subordinate; he was almost grovelling as he backed away into the other room.

Thomas thanked Rishi, who then left to join his family.

Jasmine dropped off the curried goat Thomas had ordered, and as he was tucking in, Emma arrived with her hair still wet.

"Just in time," Thomas said. "Good shower?"

"It was hot, but the pressure was low."

"Maybe I can talk to Mr. Lakhani again." Thomas explained his meeting with the minister of tourism and how they could stay longer.

Emma, disinterested in his victory, ordered the one non-Indian dish on the menu—spaghetti—and sipped her water.

"Maybe we could go to that DJ's club I told you about in a couple of days."

"I don't think I'm up for it," Emma said.

"Your stomach?"

Emma said no, it was fine. Thomas ordered another beer and they ate in silence.

Only when Jasmine returned and reminded Thomas where to meet her father the next morning to fish, did Thomas say, "I'm going fishing tomorrow. Do you want to come?"

"I came here to relax on the beach, Tom. I've never been fishing in my life. You can go if you want."

The fishing trip was brilliant. Thomas had missed the sunrise again that morning but was out on a small boat for most of the day with Jasmine's father, Adu. They shared only a handful of words from each other's language, yet he learned so much. They used both fishing nets and rods, and Thomas was thrilled he managed to catch two pomfrets by himself. Adu let him take one for supper, pointing and rubbing his stomach to indicate which of the two would be tastier.

After taking the rest of the fish to the man Adu sold them to, they stopped at the home he shared with Jasmine. Their house was modest, save for the shrine on the wall decorated with fresh flower garlands, an unlit clay lamp, and incense sticks. Outside, with a long knife Adu cleaned the fish: glittering scales flew in all directions and stuck to his dark skin like jewellery. Then he wrapped the pomfret in a newspaper for Thomas to take to Jasmine to cook.

Thomas entered their room, unwrapped the fish, and laid it out on the table for Emma to see.

Emma stared. He noticed that she was in the middle of folding her clothes into her suitcase.

"What are you doing?" she said. "That thing reeks."

"What are *you* doing?"

"Going home."

"Home? Why? You're not having a good time?"

"No. I am not having a good time. Nothing on this trip has been a good time, and I think it was a mistake."

"What happened?"

"All I wanted to do was relax on the beach. But for some reason, there were kids there today. They kept screaming *Ta-ta! Ta-ta!* It was cute the first time, but God, are those the only English words these people learn? *Ta-ta.* I ended up having to come back to our room and spend the day here. You shouldn't have left me."

"You're critiquing their English? How many Hindi words have you learned? How many words in any language have I heard you use? *Please, thank you, hello*—they go a long way." Thomas thought about Jasmine, who tried so hard to learn English, relying only on tourists and picking new words out of the air. "I mean, you haven't made the slightest attempt to embrace or even accept the culture here."

"This isn't what I thought it would be. The brochures and travel agents back home sold it as this magical, spiritual place. But they don't tell you how loud and dirty it is."

"Not spiritual? Most of the people here pray more than our priests. And how do you expect to see the magic in a place if you lock yourself in the bloody room?"

"Thomas, I'm going home."

"Then go."

"You're not coming with me?"

"You're the one who made me leave Goa and come all the way here, and now you want me to leave again and go back home before I'm ready?" Thomas turned and walked to the door.

"Take your goddamn fish with you," Emma shouted.

Thomas stomped back in, picked his fish up from the table, and carried it out in one hand. "I'm going to eat it, too!"

And he did. Thomas ate alone in the dining area, devouring the spiced and fried pomfret, picking every bit of flesh from its bones and licking his fingers afterwards. When he returned late that night, Emma was already asleep.

The birds woke Thomas early; Emma wasn't awake, but her packed bags sat beside the bedpost. He left their room and walked down to the water's edge. The sun hadn't come up yet, and the water and sand were cool on his feet.

José's tune returned to his head as he walked the shore. The morning felt pure—he was no longer thinking or searching, just walking.

And it was then, with one step in the sand, that Thomas felt something beneath his big toe. He looked down as a soft wave spread over the sand, nearly erasing his footprint. He almost kept walking, but something made him stop.

He crouched down and sifted through the mud with his fingers. He found only sand. But when a fresh wave brushed over the area, a sparkle caught his eye. And there it was. Emma's ring! Thomas plucked it out of the sand, rinsed it off, and held it in his palm.

Crouched there in the surf, he turned the ring in his fingers. He pressed its sides, testing its strength. He eyed the cut of the diamond and the smooth, simple shape of the dolphin.

On the horizon, a sliver of sun pierced the sea. The gold rose and grew and set fire to the clouds.

Thomas stood, staring at the sunrise, feeling its warmth, and let the ring fall from his fingers, into the gentle waves, to be carried out to sea.

1996

Small Things

Clara had her notes for the next day's thesis defence scattered on the dining room table. It was an hour past midnight, so it was actually *that* day's thesis defence, but Clara didn't allow herself to view it this way; it was too disheartening. The house was quiet. The rain had stopped a few hours ago, and the night outside seemed to be at rest. The silence was familiar to Clara—it was her time to study, both when she was back in India, as well as here in Canada. Three years of night classes would all come down to one evening to see if she'd be recertified to teach.

She had hoped to have more time to review, but her kids had gotten into such a hullabaloo earlier in the evening. Ally had a project due, and although Clara had taken her to the library to get books on blue whales a week and a half ago, she hadn't opened them until tonight. And Aiden had turned the house upside down packing for his school trip to Quebec. Ally didn't want him to take her CD player, so Aiden wouldn't let her use his markers to make a diagram of plankton. A shouting match ensued until Felix yelled from upstairs for the kids to behave themselves, but it was the third period of the hockey game and Clara and the kids knew it would take much more to pull him away.

From the dining room table, Clara could see Aiden's two packed bags sitting near the door; beside them, leaning against the wall, were Ally's rolled-up Bristol boards bound with elastics. She made a note to remember to pack Gravol for Aiden in the morning and another to make sure Ally didn't forget to bring her project to school. She was about to add another note to remind Felix to be home for Ally tomorrow after school, but seeing the Bristol boards reminded her of plankton. Before Ally went to bed she'd finished drawing the whale's comblike teeth that trapped krill. As Clara tucked her in, Ally asked in a halfway-to-dreaming voice, "Do whales really eat such tiny things?" Clara gave her forehead a kiss and explained that even the biggest creatures sometimes relied on small things to stay alive.

Clara yawned. The furnace came clanging to life and air hissed through the vents. She put her pen down. She was close to being done, although she needed a break, and stood up and walked three steps to the living room. She stretched her arms out to her sides, swung them up high above her head like a diver, and reached down to touch her toes. Then she stood up straight, her eyes level with the framed photo on the wall that Aiden had insisted she hang right above the couch. Goa. Towering coconut trees, the glassy ocean flirting with the sand. She closed her eyes and imagined the waves and the warm breeze tickling her skin.

The photo had been sent over by a young fellow named Thomas that Clara had met on the train during her last visit to India. She'd gone back to pay respects to her father. The stone cross on his grave had seemed so severe and final. On that trip, she'd heard from many in the village about what a great man he'd been. She knew herself how he had worked his whole life in a mill so that his children could have an education. She'd decided then that she would not waste what had been given to her. She wanted to teach. To do in Canada what she had done in India for years. To do what she loved.

In the afternoon, before her defence, Clara picked up Ally from school. Ally usually took the bus with Aiden, but he was away on his school trip. On the ride home, she told her mother how some kids in her class wouldn't believe that whales weren't fish. Clara gave Ally a rear-view-mirror smile and asked her if she'd finished her lunch.

"Everything except the banana," Ally said.

"And what did your banana learn in school today?"

"Integers. It had a big bruise on it, though."

"Maybe your banana got in a fight with its brother on the tree."

Ally crinkled her nose.

In the driveway of their home, a few puddles lingered from the previous four days of rain. Clara got out to help Ally carry her backpack and Bristol boards into the house, and gather her own notes for her thesis defence. As she slid out of the back seat, Ally pushed the car door closed with her elbow. Clara realized her keys were still in the car the moment it shut.

"Dammit!" she said, trying the handle, and ran around the car to check the other doors.

The engine hummed gently. She could see the keys in the ignition, the dangling Tweety Bird key chain swaying. Ally peeked in, too. She tried to pull open the same door, apologizing when she also found it locked. Clara breathed slowly in and out through her nose and turned to her daughter. She told Ally it wasn't her fault and that it would be okay. She went to the garage. There was a fake security sticker on the garage door, but it only creaked as she pulled it up. Then her heart dropped: there was no car inside.

"Where is your father? He should be home by now." She checked the door into the house inside the garage—locked, of course—and rejoined her daughter on the driveway. "Ally, let me have your key so we can get inside."

"I don't have my key."

"What do you mean you don't have it?"

"Aiden has it."

Clara went to try her husband at work on a neighbour's phone (no luck) and Ally checked if her friends were home (none either), and they met back at the idling black Corolla in the driveway.

"Johnny and Pearl aren't home," Ally said.

"Well, if your father doesn't get home soon, you might be coming with me to school."

"You didn't get Dad?"

"No," Clara said. "I forgot to remind him before he left for work to come straight home, but he should have known about today. Of all days!"

"We should have done like the Mathews and kept a key under our mat," said Ally. She looked at their car and said, "We can take a taxi!"

"I still need to get into the house. All my notes are in there." Clara ran her fingers through her hair and clenched it into a fist when she reached the end of the strands. "I think we need to call a tow truck," she said.

Clara went back to the neighbour's, flipped through the Yellow Pages, and found George's Automotive Service. At the bottom of the ad it said: *Locked Keys in the Car? Call Us.*

Clara gave George her address and information and asked how long it would take, explaining she was in a rush. George said, "I'll put a call in now, and Sammy should be with you shortly."

On Thursdays, Sammy broke into Olivia's apartment. Well, he didn't technically *break* in. He still had the key she'd given him when they were seeing each other; she'd overlooked asking for it back. Olivia had an odd memory like that—she forgot her bank card in the ATM occasionally, yet could tell Sammy what they had for dinner on their fifth date.

Sammy made sure nobody saw him when he entered her apartment. Olivia didn't have many friends in her building, anyway. They all lived in the city. The last time Sammy hung out with them, one guy named Charles, an accountant, made a grease-monkey joke. Sammy grabbed his shirt and told him to repeat it. Charles didn't. Sammy didn't half mind some of Olivia's co-workers at St. Augustine's Secondary where she taught history, but he didn't half like them either.

Once inside the apartment, Sammy immediately went to the windows. He was eating an apple he'd brought, and had to grip it between his teeth while he opened the blinds. By the time he got them up, enough saliva had pooled in his mouth that he had to bite off a chunk of apple before returning it to his hand. From his bag, Sammy took out the Stones' *Emotional Rescue*, put it into Olivia's CD player, and plopped onto the brown sofa.

There was something about Olivia's apartment that Sammy loved. More than just the great light and acoustics and the comfy couch, it had a *lived-in* feeling. Maybe it was the smell— like something had just been baked—or the plants in every room. The thought of getting a couple of ferns for his place briefly entered Sammy's mind, but every plant he'd ever owned had died of thirst.

Sammy closed his eyes and listened to the funky bass lines

he knew so well. For five years, he'd come to Olivia's apartment on his day off, taken a nap, and waited for her to come home. Of course, now he didn't stick around long enough to greet her when she came in, but not much else had changed. Olivia wouldn't be home for another five hours, so Sammy had plenty of time. She went to visit her mother in the old folks' home every Thursday after work. Sammy had only accompanied her a handful of times when they were together—he'd told Olivia that being around that many "coffin dodgers" made him nervous.

Sammy was awoken by a slight squeaking sound in the apartment. The album had finished and his apple core was browning on the floor. In the corner of the apartment was a small cage on the floor, where the squeaking was coming from. Olivia's gerbil, Fredrick, was running on his wheel. He must have misstepped because he went tumbling over on himself. Sammy couldn't think of a more useless pet. Groggy from his nap, he walked over to the cage and gave it a tap with his foot. Fredrick scurried into an empty toilet-paper roll.

One night when they were dating, Olivia had called Sammy in hysterics. Attracted to Fredrick's food, a mouse had squeezed right through a gap in his cage. "He's in the cage with Fredrick!" Olivia screamed down the line. "And he's not coming out." When Sammy arrived, he found the mouse huddled in one corner of the cage, Fredrick in the other, and Olivia on the far side of the apartment. She'd stacked history textbooks around the cage but left a corridor for the mouse to escape through a hole in the baseboards. Sammy rattled the cage, and the mouse zoomed right out and back into the hole, which Sammy filled with steel wool.

He went back to the couch but couldn't fall asleep again. On the side table was a framed picture of him and Olivia at

Niagara Falls, taken a half-hour before midnight on New Year's Eve. They both wore puffy winter coats, pointed hats, and toothy smiles. The falls and mist in the background were lit red, green, and blue, like painted clouds.

Sammy was surprised the picture was still out. Three weeks had passed since he and Olivia had last seen each other, and a month since the fight that ended it all. Olivia had returned from visiting her mother in the nursing home—a bad visit; her mother hadn't remembered her at all—and asked him, "Who will visit me if I ever end up like that?" Sammy didn't have an answer. She looked him in the eyes and said, "Sammy, I will love you forever," and waited. When he didn't reciprocate, she repeated more slowly, "I will love you, forever." Sammy felt trapped and said what came to him: "I love you, too, now."

He picked up the apple core from the floor and walked into the kitchen to throw it away. On the stovetop lay a crust-lined baking pan. Olivia must have made her banana bread to take for her mother. When they'd been together she used to leave a couple slices for him, and staring at the empty pan saddened him.

Sammy had met Olivia on her way back from visiting her mother, when her little red Civic got a flat tire. On his way to dinner, Sammy had noticed her pulled over on the side of the road. He told her that with all the construction it was easy for some small thing to puncture a tire. "It's my day off, but I'll help you out," he added. "You'd be my hero," she said, and when Olivia told him her name, he said olives were his favourite. After the bolts had been tightened back on and the car lowered back down, he asked if he could buy her a bite to eat. She followed him to a fish-and-chips place, and later told him that the way he'd splashed vinegar on his hands to get them clean before eating intrigued her. Later still, with their clothes scattered all over the bedroom floor, she told him he tasted salty, like an olive.

As Sammy opened the cabinet under the sink to throw out his apple core, he felt his cell phone vibrating in his front pocket.

"Sammy, it's George. Listen, the highway's a mess. A milk truck started a pileup. Nothing to cry over." Sammy heard George pause for a second to see if he was in the mood to appreciate his joke. When Sammy didn't laugh, George continued, "I'm gonna need you to take a call."

"It's my day off."

"One call—keys locked in the car. I've got all the other guys out on the highway."

George gave him the address, thanked him, and hung up. Sammy was left standing there with his apple core pinched between his thumb and index finger. George had a habit of thanking Sammy for doing something before he had a chance to refuse to do it.

Sammy opened the metal dustbin to toss in the apple core, but something caught his attention. Sitting on top of an empty bag of nacho chips was a white plastic tube shaped like a Popsicle stick, but longer and thicker. He picked it out of the can and noticed it had a display with two lines. He dug deeper into the can and found an empty box; the words *Home Pregnancy Test* took some time to process. Sammy read the instructions on the side of the box that explained what the two lines meant. Apparently, Olivia was pregnant.

Ally half-sat, half-leaned on the front bumper of the still-idling car. "We should just climb onto the garage roof and go through the window," she said.

"No thank you," said Clara. "I don't have time to wait in the emergency room." She glanced at her watch again, and then at the end of the street, simultaneously praying for the tow truck and cursing Felix. Every car that passed got her hopes up and then disappointed her. She eyed the drivers and envied how it was just a normal day for them.

"This guy is taking forever," Ally said. "If Aiden hadn't taken my CD player, I could have at least used it while we wait."

Clara gave Ally a look. But she was jumping down off the bumper.

"Look, there's a truck!"

A tow truck pulled up and a man stepped out. He walked toward them and introduced himself.

As Clara and Sammy shook hands, Ally blurted out, "You're late."

Clara put an arm around Ally and hugged her against her body.

Sammy paused and looked at Ally. He said, "I'm sorry for the delay, the highway's backed up."

"Perfect," Clara said, and pressed her lips together.

"Where you headed?"

"Mississauga."

"You could take Dundas all the way."

"I think I'll have to. If you can get this door open, you'll be our hero."

Sammy turned to the locked car, peeked inside, and felt the weather stripping along the bottom of the window. He walked back to his truck. Clara thought for a moment he might drive away, but he came back with a metal tool shaped like a paint stir stick, except longer and with a slender hook at one end.

"What is that?" Ally asked.

"It's a tool. They call it a Slim Jim."

"A Slim Jim?"

Sammy nodded, and Clara and Ally watched as he slid the

hooked end between the window and the car door. He felt around cautiously, as if he had slid his hand down there. When he wiggled the Slim Jim, the chubby golf tee of the door lock moved a little; he slowly pulled the tool up, but the lock didn't come with it. He tried twice more with the same result. He pulled the contraption out. The Toyota kept chugging exhaust into the air.

"Is it stuck?" Clara asked. She let Ally go and leaned in. She felt like taking the tool from him and trying herself.

"Just different for different cars." He slid the tool back down and tried again.

Clara wanted to take the Slim Jim and just smash the window.

Sammy wiggled the tool again but this time moved it toward the rear of the car. The lock moved up a touch at the same time.

"It's moving!" Ally shouted.

Sammy dragged it farther. The lock popped up with a gorgeous click. He slid the Slim Jim out and opened the car door.

"Yes!" Clara raised her arm in the air.

Ally clapped and said, "Hurray!" She hugged her mom, and in the excitement she turned and hugged Sammy's leg as well. Sammy leaned against the car, straightening and bending his leg like he was trying to shake off an animal. Ally let go and ran back to her mom.

Clara crouched down and asked her if she was okay.

"I'm sorry," Sammy said, stepping away from the car.

Clara told Ally to go wait on the front porch. She opened the car door all the way, reached in, and took the keys out.

She then walked past Sammy, who called out, "I don't hang around with kids much."

Clara kept going to the front door and opened it. She

brought Ally inside and closed the door behind her. She locked it.

"Why did that guy do that?" Ally asked.

"I'm not sure, sweetie." She ran her fingers through her hair. "Some people don't like to be hugged, so it's important to ask first. I think something else was going on, too." She asked Ally if she could grab her bag from the table. When the thought came to her that she still had to go write Sammy a cheque, she heard an engine start. She peeked outside and saw the truck driving away.

Sammy sat in his truck outside Olivia's apartment, right next to her parking spot. When he'd arrived, he got out of his car and walked a few steps before realizing if he wanted to talk to her, he couldn't wait in her apartment.

There were a few teenagers in the corner of the parking lot, gathered around two cars with blue lights underneath and blaring bad dance music.

Sammy honked his horn twice and stuck his arm out the window, pointing to the ground, telling them to turn down the volume. The teenagers ignored him. One of them in a tight black T-shirt and a gold chain said something to the others and they laughed.

Sammy wanted to get out of his car and teach them a lesson, but he watched the entrance, waiting to see Olivia's red Civic turn in from the street. He wasn't sure what he was going to say when she arrived. His leg still felt weird from where the kid had hugged it.

Sammy rolled up his window, but the pounding bass still infiltrated the car. The Slim Jim lay across his legs, and he pressed his thumb against the hooked end.

Sammy turned on his radio, but the clatter of a sports talk show didn't help. He shut it off. The music thumped on. He tried to watch the entrance, but the bass from the kids' music was pounding his brain.

Sammy cursed and laid on his horn.

The teenagers looked at him. The one with the chain leaned into the car and turned the music even louder. Sammy's rear-view mirror was trembling. He clenched his teeth and grabbed hold of the Slim Jim, but it wasn't until the same kid gave him the finger that he fully lost it, opened his door, and jumped out.

"Will you make it in time?" Ally asked, from the back seat.

"I should just make it," Clara said, relieved to finally be on her way. She drove faster than she normally would, but not enough to get pulled over.

As they crossed the bridge above the ravine, Ally lifted her feet up off the floor of the car. Clara didn't know where she'd picked up this superstition. She and Aiden had probably heard it was good luck. They did the same thing when driving over railway tracks; when passing graveyards, they held their breath.

When they'd cleared the bridge, Ally put her feet down, and Clara saw a red Civic swerve from the opposite lane and head diagonally into their path. Ally let out a nervous "Mom." Before Clara could even think, she was pressing the brakes to the floor. She clenched the steering wheel as hard as she could.

The Civic moved in slow motion in front of Clara. The woman inside stared straight ahead. For a long, horrifying moment it looked like they'd collide, but the rear of the red car cleared the front of Clara's car by inches. She felt her seat belt tighten across her lap and chest as they came to a screeching stop, and Clara turned in time to see a flash of red launch straight through the guardrail and out of sight. Her eyes remained fixed on that point for a few seconds, as if her mind had kept travelling forward and had to circle back to find her. When it did, she glanced back at Ally. "Honey, are you okay?"

Ally nodded, wide-eyed and clutching her seat belt.

Clara pulled the car over to the side of the road. She didn't want to get out. She didn't want to leave Ally alone in the car. She was terrified of what she might find beyond the guardrail. And yet she went. It was only many hours later, in a hospital waiting room, hearing the patient's status, that Clara was thankful she did.

So Far Away

My aunt Delilah was afraid of men. She had only arrived in Canada at the start of the summer, but it seemed longer than that. My sister and I each had our own rooms before Delilah came to live with us—Ally had to move in and share my room so Delilah could take hers. Ally's dolls and stuffed animals seemed out of place under my hockey posters and Grade 6 honour-roll plaque. We had to get bunk beds so everything could fit; I took the top bunk at first, but Ally was too scared the bed would break and she'd be crushed, so we switched.

At night, Ally and I could hear Delilah snoring through the drywall. But snoring was better than her staying awake the whole night, as she had when she first arrived. At two in the morning one night she woke up everyone in the house, shouting, "Clara! There's a man outside! Hurry, bring a stick." Everyone stumbled downstairs, half-asleep. Mom and Dad crept into the kitchen to look out into the backyard, but they saw nothing. Delilah pointed at her own reflection in the glass sliding doors. "There! Right there." Mom told Ally and me they don't have glass doors like that in Goa, and sent us back to bed. The next night Delilah thought there was a man *inside* our house. She said she had heard a noise coming from the laundry room. Our dryer was old, and the sound probably came from the vent, but Delilah thought a man was hiding in the dryer. She pressed the start button and ran. "If he's in there, let him spin."

Eventually, Delilah adjusted to our schedule. Mom helped her get a job at the pharmacy near our house. She was late for her second shift and told the pharmacist that his clock was wrong.

Mom tried to reason with her when she got back. "How can your employer's clock be wrong? That's the time you have to go by."

"The kids must have fiddled with my watch, then. It's always correct."

"I have my own watch," said Ally, and held up her arm. "A Bugs Bunny one."

"These kids have too much. Do you remember what we had back home? Spoiled rotten."

Delilah's Indian accent was much stronger than my parents', and this sounded like *rut-tin*. Ally and I thought Delilah was from another planet—we tried to avoid her after she called us that. We hoped she wouldn't get the time off work to come on vacation with us, but we were out of luck.

"Does Delilah *have* to come with us?" I asked Mom.

"Auntie Delilah. And of course she does." Delilah was the only aunt we called by her first name—I'm not sure why. She was only one year younger than my mom, who was thirty-three then, I think.

"But she'll ruin our vacation," said Ally.

Every year we rented a cottage in Sauble Beach for the August long weekend. We packed everything into the car and always left later in the morning than we'd originally planned.

We laid our comforters on the seats so that only the seat-belt clasps stuck out, put pillows behind our backs and our feet on top of coolers and suitcases packed tight with clothes. Dad drove, saying the name of every town we entered along the way—"Fergus...Arthur...Mount Forest...Durham...Dornoch"—while Mom looked at the map and passed around a Tupperware container of cut fruit. Delilah sat between Ally and me, taking up part of both our seats, and talked for most of the ride.

"I was bending down to stock the shelf, and both my knees cracked." Delilah started laughing; she always laughed before completing her stories. "And a customer said, 'Sounds like you need some WD-40.'" She tilted her head back and laughed again: a loud, knee-slapping howl. "So I asked the pharmacist if he had any WD-40 for my bones. He went searching the whole store. Until he finally asked me where I heard of it." Delilah wiped away a few tears before she continued, "That's when he told me WD-40 was mechanical oil!"

Mom laughed along with her, while Ally and I rolled our eyes and looked out the windows.

Dad slowed down the car and pointed at a big sign on the roadside. "Look, my friend Cassius owns that place. He's meeting us at the beach later today."

The sign read, *Fisherman's Paradise—40 km West of Sauble Beach*, with a giant fish leaping in the air. The fish was hooked on a line, yet still looked happy.

Jenny Wren was a small cottage tucked in among the trees on a quiet street not far from the beach. On either side were similar-sized cottages, one named Lucky Strike and the other In Debt Forever. The air smelled of pine needles and people said hello to one another walking down the street. Inside Jenny Wren, the furniture was made from logs, and you could hear chipmunks running on the roof. The two rooms were separated by wooden walls that didn't go all the way to the A-shaped ceiling: when Ally and I were younger we used to throw rolled-up socks and underwear over the walls. My parents took one bedroom and Ally and I shared the other, though the bunk beds didn't seem so special now that we had them at home. Delilah took the pullout in the living room. We unloaded the car as quickly as we could and headed to the beach. Dad stayed behind to nap, but said he'd join us soon.

Our usual spot in the sand dunes had been sectioned off with orange mesh fencing. There was a sign posted with a picture of a grey-and-white bird under the words *PIPING PLOVER, Endangered Species Nesting Grounds*. Someone had used a marker to add an "M" to the sign so it read *PIMPING PLOVER* instead.

"I've seen that bird before on my walks in the morning," said my mom. "He's a tiny fellow. Runs along the water's edge."

"I want to see it," Delilah said.

"Tomorrow morning, we'll go."

We continued down the beach and found a spot in the sand closer to the water. The sun looked lonely in the sky without clouds, though its rays warmed my skin nicely.

"Like the beaches in Goa, no?" Mom asked.

"Except no coconut trees," Delilah said.

Ally and I dropped our towels and bags and ran to the lake. We tested the temperature with our toes. It was cool at first, but we waded in. We always paused before the water reached our privates, jumping the gentle waves, afraid to take the next step. Eventually one of us splashed the other and we both went under. We swam out past the first couple of sandbars. Dad was the one to call us in if we went too far; with him still at the cottage, we stayed close to the shore. We swam for a short while, but got out as soon as Delilah came in.

"Mom, why's Delilah going in the water in her T-shirt and shorts?" Ally asked.

Mom was digging a hole for the beach umbrella. She looked up and said, "We'll have to get a bathing suit for her tomorrow. In India, people just swim in whatever they're wearing."

We watched Delilah sit in the shallow water where only young kids played.

She came running back soon after, dripping water. "The water's cold. Very cold."

"It's fine once you get in," Ally said.

"Lousy. What's the point of a beach if the water's so cold? And no salt. Vagator Beach back home is much better. Now I have to go to the toilet, it was so cold."

"The washrooms are way down there." I pointed to a small building at the end of the beach. I'd never heard someone say they have to go to the *toilet*; it sounded rude. Ally and I just peed in the lake, blaming each other for the warm spots.

"Aye sahiba," Delilah said before she turned to go.

I could hear her talking to herself as she speed-walked down the beach. Her voice trailed off, but I kept watching her. Delilah had been saying that things were better in India ever since she arrived. I had only been to India once when I was very young but didn't really want to go back—it sounded crowded and dirty.

"Why did Delilah come here, Mom?" I asked.

Mom stuck the umbrella in the hole she had dug. "Well," she said, filling the hole in with sand and patting it down, "if one of you were in a nice place, with lots of opportunity, wouldn't you want your family to be there, too?"

I nodded.

"It takes courage to come from so far away, to a place that's so different from the one you're accustomed to."

"Is she going to stay with us forever?" Ally asked.

"That's up to her."

131

My dad, wearing swimming trunks, a golf shirt, and a blue Montreal Expos hat, eventually joined us on the beach after his nap.

"I went walking, but I didn't see Cassius," he said, and sat down on a corner of the mat in the sun.

"Where did you tell him to meet you?" Mom asked. She and Delilah were sitting in the shade of the umbrella.

"The beach."

I was lying on my towel, letting the sun dry me after swimming again. Ally had made friends with a girl her age and they were drawing pictures in the sand near the water.

"You didn't tell him where to meet you? The beach is miles long," said Mom.

"What does he look like?" Delilah asked.

"He's as tall as me. From Madras but doing well for himself here. He works for the government, has a house in Mississauga and cottages he rents in Wiarton."

"Is he friendly with anyone?" Mom asked.

"Bachelor. I will introduce you, Delilah."

"Oh, no, no," Delilah said, shaking her head.

"Why not? You need to hurry, there's not much time left to start a family."

"Felix!" Mom snapped. "This isn't her last chance. Just introduce them and see if they get along. That is, if you ever find this *Cassius*." She and Delilah started laughing.

They were interrupted by a shout: "Felix!"

A man walked up wearing a Molson T-shirt and holding his sandals in one hand.

"Cassius! You found us. How ya doing?" Dad stood up and shook his hand.

"Good. Good. I recognized your hat."

"Come, meet the family. This is my wife, Clara."

"How do you do." They shook hands.

"My son, Aiden."

I sat up from my towel. Cassius looked me in the eye when he shook my hand with a tight grip. He had a nose like a parrot's beak—well, maybe not as long, but still pretty big.

"And this is my lovely sister-in-law, Delilah."

"Nice to meet you," they both said at the same time.

An awkward silence followed.

"Aiden, go fetch your sister to meet Cassius," Mom said.

I looked back to see Cassius sitting down on the mat beside Delilah. He said something to her I couldn't hear, and she tilted her head back and laughed, loud and clear, her voice ringing across the beach.

Back at the cottage, after dinner, Dad waited until Mom had gone to the corner store to ask Delilah what she'd thought of his friend.

"He seems nice," was all Delilah would say.

Cassius had left our cottage just a little while earlier—he thanked my mom and Delilah for dinner and apologized for having to run. "I have to take the guests out fishing tomorrow morning." He also invited us all to his place in Wiarton. "Come tomorrow. I insist."

Mom returned carrying a small bundle of wood and a plastic bag. "Here are the marshmallows," she said to Ally and me. "Look what I found as well, Delilah." Mom pulled a coconut from the plastic bag. "The coconut you wanted on the beach."

Delilah's eyes lit up.

"Why don't you show the kids how to break it while Felix and I clean up? There's a hammer in the drawer."

Delilah came onto the deck carrying the coconut, a hammer, a coffee mug, and a butter knife. She placed the knife and mug on the railing, then shook the coconut next to her ear. "This is a good one." She let us shake it next to our ears to hear the

133

liquid sloshing inside. "There was one riddle we used to tell back home: 'What has three eyes but cannot see?'"

Ally and I didn't answer, so Delilah continued, "It's round like the earth, a desert on the outside, an ocean on the inside." She shook the coconut again.

"A coconut?" Ally guessed.

"You got it." Delilah held the coconut in the palm of one hand like a five-pin bowling ball and rapped the centre of the shell with the hammer. Each time she hit the coconut she gave it a quarter turn in her hand, forming a line around the centre. After several knocks, liquid started to trickle out of the bottom. She quickly placed the coconut on the mug, wedged the knife into the crack, and let the water drip down inside.

"Back home, the boys climb so high, up to the top of the coconut trees. Your uncle Quinton will show you, if you go. He'll take you all around Goa on his scooter. Quinton used to climb the trees, too, but he stayed up there for such long times. That was another riddle we used to tell." Delilah let out another loud laugh. "What goes up and never comes down?"

"Quinton?" Ally guessed.

"That's what we'd say when he climbed a coconut tree, but it's not the real answer."

"Is the real answer a balloon?" Ally tried.

"No," said Delilah.

"It's smoke," I said.

"No. Think about it, and I will tell you tomorrow if you can't get it."

We each had a sip of the sweet water from the mug, then Delilah gave the coconut one more knock and it split in half. She used the butter knife to pry the white flesh from the inside of the shell and gave us small pieces.

"Eat. You kids are too skinny. Your mommy and I were the same way when we were your age. Skinny but strong. And *so young* everyone else thought we were. You kids are the same."

We nodded as we chewed. Cassius seemed to have put her in a good mood.

We saved two sips and a few pieces for Mom and Dad, and carried the coconut shell and the bag of wood to the firepit.

In the fading light, Ally and I gathered dead sticks and birchbark from the fallen trees behind the cottage. We made a teepee of sticks and inside placed the birchbark and the newspaper Dad had brought from home. Delilah lit a match to start the fire, using a large stick she found to adjust the logs. Soon we were all gathered around the crackling flames, sitting underneath a night sky crowded with stars. Delilah tossed the two halves of the coconut shell into the fire, and after a few minutes they roared to life: flames flared from the eyes of the coconut shell, like the eyes of the Devil.

With sticky marshmallow hands and heavy eyelids, we all went to bed. That night Delilah's snoring didn't stop me from falling asleep. I dreamt of climbing the tall coconut trees in India and riding my uncle's scooter.

I was awoken by Delilah's voice. It took me a while to realize she was talking in her sleep. I couldn't really make out what she was saying—most of it was in another language, but she kept repeating one name in an almost fearful voice: "Xavier, Xavier..."

"Did you see the Pimping Plover?" I asked Delilah and my mom the next morning after their walk. They had both hurried inside because it had started to rain.

"No. There were too many people out looking for him," said Delilah.

"I used to see that bird almost every morning walk here. He'd blend in with the sand and small shells, but you could usually spot him," said Mom. "Nobody cared before, but now that he's endangered everyone wants to see him. And only when he's gone will they really appreciate him."

Ally came out of the bathroom and looked out the window. "It's raining?"

"Yep. Doesn't look like we'll be going to the beach today," Mom said.

"What will we do all day then?" Ally asked.

"Do you have cards?" asked Delilah. "Come, we'll play a game."

We folded Delilah's bed back into a couch and pulled up a table and chairs. Delilah showed us how to play Devil, which turned out to be the same as Old Maid. Delilah lost the first three games in a row.

"Do you remember how Quinton used to cheat?" Delilah asked Mom. "He'd throw the Devil out with the pairs, and we'd be picking cards from each other. Picking, picking, picking, and no one had the Devil."

Dad was fiddling with the radio reception to pick up the Jays game, when we broke for lunch: pizza and samosas.

Delilah then showed us how to play Money, which was like Monopoly but with cards.

"Do you remember, Delilah, how Nunna always used to cheat at Money?" asked Mom.

"You couldn't go to the toilet, even," said Delilah. "If ever you left, Nunna would wait until you were gone, then say to the others, 'Okay, we all take one hundred, then.'"

The day passed like this: card games and comfort food and memories. The rain kept coming and didn't stop until around four. Mom and Dad went to pick up a bottle of wine for Cassius while we got ready to go. Delilah put on a blue sari and makeup.

"What goes up and never comes down, Delilah?" Ally asked.

"You figured it out?"

"No, I want you to tell us."

Delilah paused for effect, then said, "Your age."

"Ah! Should have guessed," I said.

Delilah put her makeup away and asked, "How do I look?"

"Bea-utiful," said Ally. "Are you going to marry Cassius?"

"We just met!" But then she shrugged. "Let's see what happens."

"If he catches you a fish today, I think you should," Ally said.

Delilah laughed hard but had to stop herself before she ruined her makeup.

"Who knows? Maybe I will catch a fish for him," said Delilah. "One old neighbour of ours, Xavier, he taught me to fish when I was young."

I recognized the name from last night but didn't want to let Delilah know I had heard her.

"Fantastic fisherman," she continued. "He only needed a stick, a line, and a small piece of mango skin to catch fish. He showed me how, too. I used to sneak away to his house. But don't tell Mommy. She thought I was getting tuitions for mathematics."

I wanted to ask if Xavier was still in Goa, but Delilah kept talking.

"I'll show you when we get there. Ally, go fetch that stick I used for the fire. I don't have mango, but I'll use an orange skin instead."

Cassius brought a beer for my dad and shandies for my mom and Delilah, then asked Ally and me what we wanted to drink. "Beers as well?" He ruffled my hair and pinched Ally's cheeks.

We were all seated on Cassius's deck facing the lake, with some smaller cottages clustered around. Nestled between two trees was a *Fisherman's Paradise* sign similar to the one we saw on the highway.

Cassius barbecued hamburgers and corn on the cob, served on Styrofoam plates instead of real ones. After we finished eating, he said, "Shall we move down to the dock?"

We walked across a short beach that had stones instead of sand. Delilah stopped at the car to grab her stick and orange.

"What are those for?" Cassius asked as she walked out onto the dock.

"Fishing," she replied, stepping out of her sandals.

"You aren't going to catch anything with that."

"Who said? I just need some line. I'll show you."

"There's line in that green tackle box right there, but you're better off using one of my rods."

Delilah found a spool of blue fishing line and tied it to her stick just below a knot in the wood; the end was still charred black from the night before. She tied a weight and a hook to the line, then bit off a small piece of orange peel and attached it to the hook. She threw the line in the water, staring at the brief ripples it made.

I was curious to see if Delilah's way of fishing that she'd learned from Xavier actually worked. Mom, Dad, Ally, and I sat in lawn chairs on the dock and watched. The mosquitoes had just begun to come out.

"Well, if you're fishing, I might as well join you." Cassius grabbed an expensive-looking rod from the rowboat tied to the dock. From a coffee can full of soil he found a fat worm, took out a red Swiss Army knife from his pocket, and sliced the worm in two.

"How many tools does that knife have?" my dad asked.

"Fifteen. Screwdriver, file, saw...you name it. My father gave me this knife," Cassius said.

I wanted to see all the tools fold out, but Cassius put the knife back into his pocket. He tossed one half of the squirming worm back into the coffee can and poked a hook through the other half. With a quick flick of his wrist, he cast his line out much farther than Delilah's.

Cassius got a few nibbles right away but didn't catch anything. He and Delilah both threw their lines out again. And then many more times after that. It was like they were fishing for gold.

"You sure you don't want some real bait?" Cassius asked.

"I'm fine," Delilah replied.

A moment later Cassius said, "Your weight is too heavy. Nothing's going to bite that deep."

"Just wait, Baba," Delilah said.

My mom and dad exchanged a look. Cassius and Delilah sounded like an old married couple.

Ally and I were going to head back to the beach to skip stones, but Cassius's line went tight and the rod bent down.

"Oh yeah!" he shouted, reeling in the fish like an expert. Cassius pulled the fish out of the water and said, "Rainbow trout. A beauty." The fish was frantic, flopping back and forth on the dock. Cassius grabbed hold of it tightly and it stopped flailing.

It was a medium-sized fish, but a good-looking one, with a spotted back and pink stripes down its sides. Cassius took a pair of pliers from the tackle box, removed the hook from the fish's mouth, and held it up with both hands to show everyone. The fish gasped for breath, drowning in the air; the way it opened and closed its mouth, it looked like it was trying to say something. Cassius let Ally and me touch the trout's skin, which was surprisingly smooth—both soft and firm at the same time.

Mom didn't touch it, but said, "It's a very nice fish."

Delilah stayed at the end of the dock rolling in her line.

Cassius asked my dad to open the cooler before he slid his catch in and snapped the lid shut. "Tell ya what, Felix, why don't you take this one home with you?"

"Yeah?" my dad said.

"Sure. Have him for lunch tomorrow. A little butter, fry him up, and you're golden."

"Thanks, Cassius," Dad said.

"No problem. You know how to clean it, right?"

"I'm sure the wife does," Dad said. He smiled at Mom with playful eyes.

"No thank you." Mom gave him a light whack on the shoulder. "That's one job I could never stomach."

"How about you, Delilah? You clean fish, right?" Cassius asked.

"Only ones I catch myself." Delilah threw her line back out.

"Well, I'm good for the day," Cassius said, but when he saw Delilah was still trying, he cast his line out again.

As the pair continued their back-and-forth teasing, the light turned dim, and I wondered when the competition would end. I wanted Delilah to catch something, even a small fish. She looked so out of place standing there in a sari, fishing barefoot off the dock.

And then her line wiggled. She pulled up slowly. Gave it a little tug.

"Probably a boot," Cassius teased, but Delilah kept her concentration.

A second later her line ran sharply to the right, knocking her off-balance. "Arrey!" Delilah shouted. She regained her footing and turned the stick sideways with a hand on each end, like she was water-skiing behind a fast boat.

We cheered her on, not wanting the fish to get away. To reel it in, she rolled the stick in her hands. I was worried it might break, but she had clearly done this many times. The line became shorter and shorter, until she yanked the fish out of the water like a stubborn weed from the ground. The smile on her face when she pulled it out was pure joy.

It was the biggest, ugliest fish I had ever seen. Dark grey, the fish had a flat head, small eyes, and whiskers on its face like a dirty old man.

Delilah still held the stick with both hands. The fish didn't fight at all once out of the water—it stayed so still that it spun slowly as the line untwisted.

"You should throw that thing back," Cassius said.

"Throw it back? Why?" Delilah asked.

"It's a catfish."

"So? We'll fry this one as well."

"You don't want to eat that. If you had caught a salmon or trout, I'd say keep it. But a catfish?"

"You're just jealous it's bigger than your fish."

"Trust me, you don't want that thing." Cassius took out his Swiss Army knife. He grabbed the line with one hand and put the knife against it with the other. Making a loop, he forced the knife sideways and the line cut. The catfish fell, bounced off the edge of the dock, and plunked back into the water.

"Idiot," said Delilah and, before any of us knew what was happening, she pushed Cassius off the dock.

He hit the water with a splash a hundred times larger than the catfish's. Delilah threw her fishing stick in after him, too, and it bobbed near his head when he came up. Cassius's eyes were wide. He pulled himself up onto the dock, clothes dripping water. He stood there for a moment, then said, "My knife!" and jumped back into the lake.

All of us except Delilah moved to the edge of the dock to help search for the knife. But the light was too dim and the water too deep and murky to see anything.

"Cassius, I'm sorry," Dad said.

"Delilah, what were you thinking?" Mom asked.

Delilah had already put her sandals back on and was sitting in a chair at the base of the dock with her orange. She peeled the rest, throwing the skin in the water, and ate it one slice at a time.

Cassius climbed out of the water and trudged back along the dock, wetting the wood as he walked. He continued past the beach and back into his cottage without saying a word.

Mom turned to Delilah with angry eyes. But a bang sounded across the lake and a lone firecracker exploded high above. A string of explosions followed—like big spiders, the yellows, reds, and blues reflected on the rippling water.

The display continued long enough for Cassius to rejoin us in dry clothes.

Then it was over. I kept expecting another firecracker, and when it didn't come, the lake looked so dark. Somewhere in there was Delilah's fish.

Dad decided we should get going and turned to Cassius. In a low voice, but not so low that we couldn't hear, he said, "Thanks for having us. And sorry again about Delilah."

"Yes, and I hope you find your knife," Mom added.

As we were getting in our car, Cassius ran up with the fish he'd caught in a grocery bag. He placed the bag between my feet in the back seat of the car, ruffled my hair, and said, "Take care of this one."

I didn't smile back at him before he shut the door. And Delilah just sat there, staring out the windshield, saying nothing.

The street lamps were far apart on the country road—as we drove between them, it felt like only the car's headlights were defending us from the darkness all around.

"You shouldn't have pushed him in," Mom said.

"He cut my line," Delilah said.

"Regardless, you don't go to someone's place and push them in the lake."

"Cassius isn't likely to invite us there again," Dad added, looking in the rear-view mirror. "You had a shot."

"I wouldn't want to marry that gunda," said Delilah.

The plastic bag at my feet rustled and went still. The whole ride home I kept picturing the fish flopping on the dock, trying to swim and breathe out of water.

The next morning, Delilah cleaned and cut the fish for lunch. She did it so quickly and easily that I thought she enjoyed it at first. But once the fillets were cooked and we sat down to eat, she refused to taste even one bite. She just sat there as she had in the back of the car, staring into the distance, not saying a word.

Shortly after Ally and I started the new school year, Delilah flew back to Mumbai.

"I thought it would be the winter that would give her trouble," Mom said. "But she didn't even get to see the snow."

Ally moved back into her old room again, taking the top bunk with her and making my bed a normal one. At night, it felt strange to not hear Delilah's snoring in the next room. Ally and I tried playing the games Delilah had taught us, but it wasn't the same without her stories and riddles.

"Will Delilah ever come back?" I asked Mom.

"I don't know," Mom said. "Maybe you can go visit her when you're older."

"I will, one day," I said. "I'll climb the coconut trees in Goa and ride all around on Uncle Quinton's scooter. Is Xavier still there, too?"

"Xavier?" Mom's face turned sour almost immediately. "I haven't heard that name in years. Did Delilah tell you about Xavier?"

I remembered then that Delilah had said not to mention Xavier to Mom, but I didn't think she would get in trouble after all these years for skipping her tuitions to go fishing. I nodded to my mom.

"She should not have told you." She clicked her tongue once and shook her head back and forth. "But you shouldn't worry, he's not there anymore to hurt children. They chased that Devil out of our village long back."

I felt like something I'd eaten had gone rotten, but only after it was inside me. I tried my best to bury that feeling, as deep down as I could, but from time to time it showed its ugly head. And yet I still kept hoping that, one day, I would have the courage to go to a place so different, and so far away.

Fallen Leaves

Ricky's dog Chaos was as big as a lion and as dumb as a turkey. She was a black Russian terrier, taller while on all fours than any of us standing, and weighing more than Ricky, me, and Johnny put together. When we rang Ricky's doorbell, we'd hear Chaos run down the hallway, barking like a banshee, her nails clicking on the tiles. She would jump up with such force that the door moved in its frame. But as soon as she recognized our scents, she went back to her gentle ways, and when the door was opened she often begged to be scratched behind her ears or on the forehead. I always wondered how she could see with so much shaggy hair over her eyes—maybe that's why she was so clumsy.

One fall day, Ricky rang my doorbell early for a Saturday morning. I was halfway done my bowl of Cheerios with a banana sliced in, but scarfed down the rest when he promised a surprise. The last time Ricky said he had a surprise, he led us to a giant trampoline in his backyard—a friend of his father's had loaned it to them for a week while he was away. We jumped on that thing for two whole days straight. I'm pretty sure we were jumping in our dreams as well. On the third day, Johnny got double-bounced too high and broke his collarbone on the way down. We weren't allowed on the trampoline after that; it sat unused for the rest of the week and a faded patch of grass was left when it was taken away.

On this Saturday morning, I was less excited when I saw Ricky was bringing Chaos with us, but I didn't say anything. We called on Johnny and grabbed our bikes.

Ricky led the way on a forest trail not far from our homes. I rode behind him, and Johnny followed me. As we pedalled, Chaos galloped alongside us and we tried not to get bumped as she slowed down to sniff the ground and trees, then ran hard to catch up to Ricky.

Johnny kept calling out, asking what surprise Ricky had in store. But Ricky wouldn't say.

I squeezed my bike brakes gently as Ricky came to a stop. I was riding Johnny's old bike and only the front brake worked, so I had to be careful or I'd get thrown forward. Johnny had just gotten a new eighteen-speed for his birthday at the start of the school year; only his tiptoes touched the ground if he took his feet off the pedals.

"Chaos! Where you going?" shouted Ricky after the dog, who had run off the path and into the forest. She stopped and shook her head back and forth.

A few seconds passed before we realized she had got hold of something. We jumped off our bikes and ran, shouting at Chaos to put down whatever she had, but we arrived too late. She dropped a grey squirrel, torn to tufts of bloody fur, its insides outside.

"Poor thing's finished," I said, and turned away from the small corpse.

"Yeah, she mangled it," said Johnny. "Was probably just out hiding nuts before it gets cold."

146

"Bad girl! What got into ya?" Ricky shouted, and attached a leash to her collar. Chaos lowered her head and gave us an almost shameful look. "I've never seen her do anything like that. Something must have spooked her." Ricky spooked me when he said this, and I wondered if Chaos sensed what I'd found out the night before about her from Ricky's father.

We left the squirrel lying there and walked our bikes the rest of the trail until we reached a clearing. When we got to the nice baseball diamonds, Johnny got off his bike and pretended to crank a game-winning home run. These fields had green grass, painted lines, and lights for night games, while the field near our house was mostly dirt, and before playing we had to draw the bases with the heels of our shoes.

Ricky pedalled a bit farther, staring at a small stall that sold candy and refreshments during the games. A moment later I noticed what he was staring at. The window had a locked metal cover, but the back door stood slightly ajar. I watched him tie Chaos to his bike and walk toward the door. He peeked in, then swung the door wide open and entered the stall. Johnny and I exchanged looks and followed him.

There for the taking was every kid's dream: chocolate bars, chips, gum, and candy—soft candy, hard candy, sweet, sour, and salty candy.

"When did you find out about this?" asked Johnny.

"Right now. This isn't what I wanted to show you guys, but it's even better!" Ricky smiled, grabbing a fistful of gumball packets and shoving them into his jean pocket. Johnny and I looked at each other. I peeked out the door again to see if anyone was around; Chaos still sat tied to Ricky's bike, but I saw no one else. Johnny popped a purple jawbreaker into his mouth, but it was too big and his cheek bulged out like a squirrel's.

"I don't know if we should, Ricky," I said.

"C'mon, man, nothing's gonna happen. We gotta hurry up,

though," said Ricky, as he stuffed chocolate bars into his pockets. I had never stolen something so big. The only thing I ever took was bracelet beads at summer day camp, and that wasn't really stealing. My sister and I were making bracelets and didn't finish in time. We wanted to take some beads home but didn't want to ask for them, so we poured handfuls into our socks so no one would see. The beads started off around our ankles but soon leaked down beneath our feet. Our dad picked us up that day, although instead of going home he took us along to buy groceries. As Dad put items into the cart, my sister and I tried to walk down the aisles normally, but the beads were pressing against our feet and rolling between our toes. Dad didn't notice. When we got home we went to my room, covered the floor with paper, and carefully pulled our socks off and brushed the beads from our feet. We'd felt so smart that day, yet for some reason taking candy felt different.

Still, I picked up a box of Smarties and put it in my right pocket. After that it was easier to take more. We each grabbed one more bag of chips than our arms could carry, and we kept having to stop and pick them up on our way out the door. We folded our shirts up to hold everything, picked up our bikes with our free hand, and ran alongside them as best we could. I could feel the box of Smarties in my pocket rattle, but I joined my friends' laughter because we'd gotten away with it.

Johnny and I had been so busy opening packages and eating that we didn't notice Ricky's surprise until we were right in front of it. He pointed ahead and we saw the leaves. Lots and lots of leaves—piled as high as a house and a mix of red, yellow, and orange. In our neighbourhood, the townhouses didn't have many tall trees. Our front yard had only a single skinny tree that stood alone like an upside-down broomstick. Mom always joked that "a witch must have crash-landed there." She didn't like that tree—"No shade, no fruit, no nice flowers," she'd say. Dad liked it because it was the first one he had bought in Canada.

The leaves piled up here must have come from the houses by the lake. There, they had giant houses with giant trees that no one sat under or climbed.

We dropped our haul of stolen candy and climbed, jumping and pushing one another in the rich people's leaves. We laughed at the wealth they were unaware they had thrown away, and tossed their leaves in the air like lottery money. We were drunk off the cool air, fallen leaves, and sugar, yet kept returning to the bottom of the leaf pile to eat more candy, throwing the wrappers in the rusted garbage can with no bag.

Ricky got Chaos to climb the leaf mountain and had the idea to set a trap for her. As much as he loved his dog, he teased her mercilessly. Every time we'd take her out to do her business on the hill behind Ricky's house, we'd play a trick on her. For some reason, Chaos would only crap at the bottom of the hill, right beside the creek. We'd wait until she started going down the hill and then run away as fast as we could and hide from her. After she was finished, she used her nose to find us, no matter where we hid.

Now we dug a hole in the leaf pile the size of a grave. The leaves on top were dry, but they got damper the deeper we dug. When we finished the hole, we lay branches across it, then covered the branches over with leaves. Chaos had seen us dig the hole and cover it up, but when we called her over from the other side, she still came barrelling over and fell right in. After she jumped out, Chaos ran back down the hill and straight into the woods. Ricky said she'd come back, so we let her go, but I wasn't so sure.

The night before, I'd overhead Ricky's dad and my parents talk in our living room over a cup of tea in that tone adults take on when they're making tough decisions. Ricky's older sister had been home from school since she'd gotten pregnant a while back. I could tell my parents still didn't approve of her and her "situation," but they sent over a dish of butter chicken the day the new baby girl, Serena, was born. Ricky's dad explained to my parents, "With the baby, our small house has suddenly become too small, and Chaos, suddenly too big." He told them how he tried to give Chaos away but no one would take a dog of her size. She wasn't always this large; they'd rescued her as a puppy, and she'd been growing ever since. She definitely stood out in the neighbourhood; all the other families had less distinct dogs. Ricky had tried to teach her tricks since the day they got her, but she only mastered a few. I often saw him in his backyard still trying to get her to play dead or roll over, without success. I wanted to tell Ricky what his father had told my parents but hadn't been able to yet.

"Chaos!" Ricky called from the top of the leaf pile, but she wasn't coming back from the woods. We were about to go look for her, when Johnny spotted a man in the distance walking in our direction. His stride suggested that he had a purpose, but it wasn't until the man got closer and looked down into the garbage can that I knew he knew.

When he glanced up at us, Ricky said, "Hide!" We scrambled over the other side of the heap of leaves so he couldn't see us. But when we peeked over, he was making his way to our bikes. He picked up Johnny's new bike by the handlebars and started to walk it away.

"Hey!" Johnny shouted to the man, but he continued walking.

We climbed over the top and ran down the mound of leaves to go after him.

"What are you doing?" Johnny asked the man when we had almost caught up.

The man stopped and turned to us. He wore a red flannel

shirt and blue jeans; his brown hair was slicked back and he had a thick moustache that didn't look right on his skinny face.

"What am *I* doing? I thought I'd take something that wasn't mine, just like you kids did."

"What are you talking about? Give me back my bike, you asshole." Johnny surprised me—he almost never swore.

"Call me that again, kid." The man stared Johnny down.

When Johnny didn't repeat his insult, he said, "That's right." The man then looked at me when he said, "You're not getting anything back until you admit what you did."

"What do you care?" Ricky asked.

The man's one fist was clenched tight and there was a vein on his forehead.

"Let's just go, guys," I said to Johnny and Ricky.

"I'm not going anywhere without my bike," Johnny said to me, but also to the man.

"How do you even know it was us?" Ricky added. "You can't prove anything."

"Well, why don't I just call the police? See what they think about your little theft."

"You call the cops and we'll tell them you tried to steal Johnny's bike," said Ricky.

I could tell the man was stumped but didn't want to let us get away. I hadn't said anything to him yet, but he turned to me and said, "This was your idea, wasn't it?" His eyes held so much hate.

I managed to shake my head, but it wasn't enough. The man rolled the bike toward us and grabbed me by the back of my neck. I tried to slip free, but he squeezed harder, and I froze. I wanted to tell him he had it wrong, that Ricky had convinced me to do it, that I wouldn't have taken anything if I were alone, but I couldn't.

"What are you doing? Let him go!" Johnny shouted.

The man held me tight. He must have been a chain-smoker; the filthy smell was in his shirt. "You kids should stay away from this boy, you hear?" he said. "These people, these people with permanent tans, they're a bad influence on normal kids. A bad influence. They shouldn't be allowed in our country, but the government lets them in, anyway. But that's okay—once the courts hear what you did they'll deport you, kid."

I heard a bark from the forest, but it was muffled and far away.

"Let him go," Johnny pleaded again. "You can take the bike."

The man held steady.

Ricky stepped closer to us and said, "Okay, we get it. We did it, just let him go."

The man grinned. "Now, you tell me that this boy made you do what you did and you can go home."

Ricky paused for what seemed like a long time. He had an empty stare, as if he was looking straight through the man.

"Well, kid, what's it gonna be?"

"Fuck you."

The man backhanded Ricky full in the face. Ricky stayed on his feet but brought his hand to his cheek and looked past us again. His eyes widened, but he didn't have time to move.

Chaos hit the man so hard, all three of us got knocked over. She clamped her teeth onto the man's leg and shook him violently.

It was not until Chaos took aim at the man's throat that we shouted at her to stop. We tried to push and pull her off him but were knocked back each time.

The man fought back, rolled and punched, kicked and cursed.

Johnny said, "Let's go," and we were on our bikes, pedalling away. Ricky kept shouting for Chaos to come to him, but she didn't listen and we kept getting farther away.

Every so often, I ask Johnny if he remembers that day. "Of course," he says, and we recount the events that led up to the fight again. I still remember the stack of leaves, and the man and dog we left beside them. Our town paper said the man had a wife and a son, but I can't imagine him with either. I remember how he'd singled me out, how his eyes burned and his words cut. Ricky never talks about that day, of course. We still shoot hoops in the summer and play street hockey when it gets cold, but I have to be careful what I say to him. He seemed to grow up overnight when they put Chaos down. There was nothing else to do. I knew it wasn't my fault, and yet I still felt guilty I didn't tell him about Chaos. I now know how lucky I was, how lucky we all were, to be shown loyalty like that. But I remember that day well. I recall the colour of the leaves, and the soft, crunching sound they made beneath our feet as we raced up the pile.

1997

One Hundred Steps

Most of the families attending the picnic were from the city, but some came from beyond, packed into cars with more passengers than seat belts. Children sat on laps, shifted from one car pool to the next, so everyone could fit. At the park, they gathered under a sign strung between two trees: *Hamilton Goan Association*. Long lines of picnic tables were adorned with plastic sheets and silver haandis, pots as large as witches' cauldrons. Curries, cutlery, and chatter were shared by all. Triangle-cut chutney sandwiches—with fresh green coriander filling—went as quickly as the samosas wrapped in oil-spotted newspaper. The most desired dish of the day was Ally's uncle Francis's pork, spiced with a potent masala and heated on a three-legged grill so the smoky flavour could permeate the fatty meat. Francis and Ally's father were lucky to still have their thick eyebrows, so thoroughly had they soaked the coals in lighter fluid before throwing in a match.

Once everyone had served themselves, Ally and her uncle sat at the far end of the picnic tables, near the shallow stream where some younger kids were trying to catch crayfish. Francis wasn't her blood uncle, but at picnics everyone became either an uncle, aunt, or cousin. Ally wore a yellow dress with white frills; Francis was underdressed, for him, in a sky-blue cotton dress shirt that didn't hide his paunch, as well as his normal suit jacket.

"One hundred steps," Ally said, gazing at the hill that rose over the park.

"That's right, kiddo."

"What's at the top?"

"Well, some say a unicorn might live up there."

"A unicorn?" Ally said, with less enthusiasm.

"That's what I heard. Though the *really* smart people know that it's a dragon."

"A dragon!" Ally's face lit up again.

"Yes, Rajesh has been there for years."

"Rajesh?"

"Yes, the dragon."

"A dragon can't be named Rajesh!"

"I wouldn't tell that to Rajesh. He's got razor-sharp teeth, thick dry scales, and he could roast you and me both with one breath. But there's really only one way to know for sure."

"Climb up?"

"You got it, kiddo."

"Let's go!" At school, Ally got in trouble for daydreaming and was often snapped back to reality by an angry teacher. But it felt different with Francis. "I have to tell Mom first," she added.

Francis stood, brushing his hands off on his pants. "Tell her we're off on an adventure."

"Eighty-eight, two fat ladies, O-88," called the bingo announcer, a man with thinning grey hair and thick glasses, from his place atop a picnic table. All of those who played sat on the tables and grass shaded by a giant maple tree. The adults had debated

how old the tree was, but they could only agree that it must be over a century. The kids loved to throw its seeds in the air and watch them propeller down like little helicopters.

"But bingo just started," Ally's mother told her and Francis. "*Jaldi-five*, I've got cards for you both." She held five thin paper cards; instead of a pen she had a small stick to poke holes through the numbers as they were called.

"*Please*, Mom, I never win at bingo, anyway," said Ally. She had enjoyed the earlier games of Seven Tiles and the water-balloon toss, but, like the older kids with their Pink Floyd T-shirts and Reebok pumps, who had already escaped, she hoped she could get away before the adults started to sing.

"She'll be back in one piece, Clara," promised Francis. He produced a maroon-and-gold pen from his shirt pocket and handed it to Ally's mother.

"Thank you, Francis. How were things at Bombay Jewel and Gem this trip?"

"Gem and Jewel," he said.

"Oh yes, I'm sorry. I'll never get that right."

"No problem... Business is *fan*-tastic. We've opened up a new storefront in Bandra and secured another contract from Germany. Busy, as always."

"*My age*," said the caller. "*Thirty, I-30.*"

Clara marked two cards and touched the bump of her belly.

"Clara, you must forgive me. I've completely forgotten to say congratulations! How much time till the next one arrives?"

"The baby is coming in February," Ally piped up. She ran her hand through her mother's long jet-black hair that fell just above her bum.

"Clara, you are truly blessed."

"*Three and a seven, N-37.*"

Clara thanked Francis and asked Ally where Aiden and her father were.

"Aiden's playing baseball with the new bat and glove Uncle bought him. Dad went, too." Ally touched the thin gold cross that Francis had brought for her. She liked it but was annoyed that her dad wouldn't let her play baseball because, he said, she was too young and might get hurt.

"Honestly, Francis, you don't need to bring the kids gifts every time."

"I missed Christmas this year. And besides, I'm happy to provide them a glimpse of the finer things in life."

"You mean spoil them," Clara replied.

"*First place, number 1, B-1.*"

Ally pointed out the cards with ones and thirty-sevens, and her mom let her take the pen and go to work.

Clara said to Francis, "If only you'd let me set you up with someone. How many times have I tried over the years?"

"You know I wouldn't have time for that."

"Yes, I remember. I recently heard a rumour, though, from some of the older ladies. According to them, you might now have a sweet jalebi back home you are friendly with."

"You know how they gossip. My only indulgence has been my business."

"How long has it been now?"

"Eighteen years. To think it all started in that cramped Bombay second-floor apartment. You could hear the traffic most of the day. Do you remember that place? You used to meet me there and we'd go for falooda near the beach at Chaupati."

"That was a long time ago."

"Yes, before Felix left the priesthood, of course." Francis placed a hand on her shoulder and gave it a gentle squeeze. Clara glanced at his hand, and he removed it.

"*O-72, my wife's age.*"

Ally, bored of the adults' talk, switched her attention to an upturned bee on the table. The bee tried twice to flip over.

Once right side up, it did not fly away but dragged itself around like an injured soldier.

"What have we got here?" asked Francis. "Poor guy's struggling, ain't he?"

"Yeah, he looks hurt," said Ally.

"Careful! It'll get up and sting you," Clara said.

"Oh, these guys are harmless if you don't give them trouble," said Francis. "Besides, this one looks pooped. Must be a scout."

He grabbed a sugar packet leftover from the thermos tea, pinched one side, gave it a shake, then ripped off a corner and poured a pimple-sized pile close to the struggling insect. Ally loved how Francis cared for all living creatures, big or small. Her parents didn't have much appreciation for animals. When she had asked her mom if she could get a cat last year, she got a lecture on how filthy they were. Ally had had to settle for a purple Siamese fighting fish she named Cat.

The bee crawled toward the sweet gift from the heavens and sucked down as much as he could; the rest, Ally knew, would be stored in the backpacks on his legs. Then he took off and flew high up and out of sight.

"B-11, take me to heaven."

"So, can I go, Mom?"

"Alright. But if you two aren't back by three, I'm sending out the search party."

On the way to the one hundred steps, Ally and Francis stopped for ice cream. At the park's lone building, a concession kiosk, Ally chose bubble-gum flavour, her favourite because it reminded her of rainbows, while Francis went with vanilla. He paid the additional seventy-five cents each for a waffle cone, and the girl at the shop gave Ally an extra scoop for free.

The cold treat was extra satisfying on the sweltering summer afternoon as they made their way to the stairway, where branches hid the entrance from all but those who knew the way. Francis held back the branches and set foot on the first of the old steps, which were covered in green moss and rounded from wear. Ally couldn't see the top as the stairs peaked and curved and faded into green.

"One...two...three...four...five." Ally counted the steps aloud as they climbed, but stopped when she felt a stream of melted ice cream on her hand. She lapped up the mix of blue, red, and purple. From then on, she counted the steps in her head, her mouth busy with ice cream; she finished it at step twenty-seven. Some steps were quite steep, but Ally, despite her skinny legs and flip-flops, powered ahead, while Francis was already struggling. At step forty, he stopped to catch his breath.

"Oh, man. Your uncle hasn't climbed one hundred steps...in a long time." His breathing was heavy and laboured, his face red. "Let's take a rest for a moment."

The trees all around shaded them from the sun, but Ally still wished she had another ice cream to cool off. She listened as the birds took turns singing solos.

"So, what are they teaching you in school these days, kiddo?"

"It's summer vacation," she said.

"Oh yes. I mean, have they taught you how plants get energy yet?"

"Photosynthesis, Uncle. Plants make energy from the sun and then only need water and soil. And then insects and animals eat the plants and then bigger animals eat them—it's the food chain." Ally bent her elbow back and forth while she spoke; she had a small blue Band-Aid with the Tasmanian Devil on it.

"Smart cookie." Francis started climbing again but stumbled and took the next couple of steps hastily.

"I told Mom about the food chain," Ally said, following him cautiously, "although she still gets mad at the rabbits for eating her tomatoes."

"Rabbits. Hmm, something tells me it could be a dragon."

"Dragons like tomatoes?"

"Vegetarian dragons do."

"Dragons aren't vegetarian."

"Some are, just like humans. They love tomatoes, and cauliflower, and strawberries."

"What about beets?"

"Roasted beets are their favourite."

"Mine, too! Is the dragon at the top of the steps vegetarian?"

"Rajesh? You know, I think he just might be."

Ally looked up at a small patch of sky visible between the trees. She pointed and said, "There he is!"

"Who?"

"Rajesh!"

"You saw him?"

"Yes, in between the clouds."

"Did he have a long tail and yellow eye?"

"Yeah, he was flying fast."

"That's Rajesh, all right."

"I hope he's at the top when we get there. We should tell Rajesh a secret so he comes back. Dragons love secrets."

"They sure do." Francis turned back and stared at Ally. "You know what? You have your mother's eyes, exactly."

People had told Ally she looked like her mother before, but it felt like more of a compliment when Francis said it.

"You make sure you don't turn into an old fart like me who works and works and works." He paused again—step fifty-two. "Do you want to know a secret?"

"Sure," said Ally, but she didn't mention that she wasn't the best person to tell secrets to because she let them out sometimes, but only by accident.

"I'm going to sell my business." Francis straightened his back and put his hands on his hips.

"Yeah?"

"No kidding. I've put a lot of thought into it, and it's the right time. Bombay Gem and Jewel has taken up too much of my life."

They resumed their climb at a steady pace, as if Francis had gotten lighter after having shared his secret.

"Will you live here the whole year round now like everyone else?"

"That's right, the whole year round."

"Will you come on my field trips next year?"

"Of course I will," Francis said, wiping the sweat from his brow. "I'm going to put my time toward family. Including starting my own."

Ally was quiet as they climbed further. She had pocketed a sugar packet after what had happened with the bee in case they ran into another one. She held on to it tightly now.

Francis continued: "I met a girl on my last trip. I've already had discussions with her family and know they'd accept a proposal. You see, starting a family is much like cutting stones. I start with something raw that needs to be shaped. I always have an end state in mind. I cut and polish, cut and polish. Step by step, I make the stone precious. Not just precious, but perfect."

Ally wasn't sure what to say. She wanted him to go back to talking about the dragons.

The sweat now made dark spots on the underarms of Francis's shirt. The birds, Ally noticed, had gone silent.

They were on step seventy-four when Francis stopped mid-stride and clutched his chest. He staggered forward and managed to brace his fall on a step that was nothing more than dirt and the root of a tree, and eased himself onto his back.

"Uncle?" Ally pulled her hand out of her pocket, and the sugar packet fell to the ground, but she stepped closer to Francis. "Are you okay, Uncle?"

"I'm fine. Just a bit of a struggle." Francis clenched his teeth and took deep breaths.

"Are you sure?"

"I'm fine. Just very tired."

Except he cried out and buried his head in the crook of his elbow. Ally had to jump out of the way when he kicked his right leg out straight and bent it back slowly. From then on, she kept her distance.

"I'm okay," he wheezed. "Ally, why don't you go on ahead and I'll be right behind you."

"Maybe I should wait with you?"

"No, I just need a bit of time. Go ahead, sweetie. I'll see you at the top." Francis gestured up the hill with a half-raised arm.

Ally didn't move.

Francis propped himself up and glared at her, shouting, "I'll be right behind you!" His eyes were fierce.

Ally turned and fled, taking steps two at a time.

As she climbed, the sun began to emerge above the treeline. Ally looked back but could no longer see her uncle lying there just off the path. She kept going, all the way to the top.

Then the path opened up. There was a park surrounded by trees, with an old playground. Ally, all alone, tried to turn the rusty merry-go-round, but it made an awful screeching noise. Across the playground was a tall, narrow slide and see-saw horses, with grins larger than any horse would make. She went over to the swing set and sat and waited, rocking on her heels, watching the clouds drift past slowly overhead.

Private Property

Before leaving for vacation, we'd gone to play hide-and-go-seek in the new subdivision of half-built houses, and construction workers had chased us away. As grizzled and manly as they were, they weren't the quickest with their heavy boots and big bellies, and we escaped without being caught. So when Ally and I came back from Sauble Beach, we waited until the construction workers had gone home, rounded up our neighbourhood friends, and headed over there.

There were seven of us: Johnny, Pearl, and I were the oldest at thirteen, and then Ricky, Steven, Jen, all twelve, and Ally, the youngest, at ten. As a group we snuck past the *Private Property* sign and onto Emperor Drive, where the houses were in various stages of construction. Some were empty concrete caverns of would-be basements, others just wooden frames that grew out of the ground like two-by-four skeletons, and then there were those that had been bricked and shingled but their insides were still bare. They were all massive, some bigger than our entire row of town homes.

"The one with the double garage is gonna be mine one day,"

Johnny said. "I'll need the space for both my Ferraris when I'm a millionaire."

"I'll live in the one beside it," I said. "We can combine our backyards and make a soccer field."

"Ally, we can take the ones across the street," Pearl said. "And put a big pool in the backyard."

"Will we still play hide-and-go-seek?" Ally asked.

"*Of course* we will," Pearl said.

There were so many hiding spots that we had to set a boundary. "Let's keep it to these six houses," I said, indicating a block.

Everyone put their hands in a circle, and Ricky counted off each of our hands to see who was It. "Inky pinky ponky, Daddy bought a donkey..." I got out first. "Ibble ubble black bubble, ibble ubble out." Then Ally, then Pearl, and everyone else, until Johnny was left with his eyes closed counting to one hundred while we all ran away to hide.

We ran past the houses that were just piles of brick, tile, shingle, and pipe. And past the house where Johnny had once found a *Playboy* magazine. That had been the first time I'd seen between a woman's legs; it looked dark and hairy and mysterious. I felt like we shouldn't be looking at the magazine, but I didn't stop Johnny from bringing it home that day. He hid it underneath a slab of patio stone at the side of his house, and we went to look at it every day for three days straight. Pearl caught Ricky and me on the third day but promised not to tell on us. She seemed curious as well and kept glancing at me while we flipped through the pages. Our eyes met once, but I got nervous and looked down at the naked woman stretched out on the deck of a boat. The magazine disappeared a couple of days later. Ricky and Johnny accused each other of stealing it and stopped talking until two days later, when we all went swimming at the public pool.

Once we were past the *Playboy* house, the six of us stopped to catch our breath before we split up to hide. I asked Ally if she was coming with me.

"No, I can find my own spot," she said, and took off in between two houses.

I watched her go, feeling anxious. The summer before, Johnny had stepped on a nail. He blamed the workers, saying it was "shoddy workmanship" to leave a nail sticking out like that, a phrase he stole from his dad. But I didn't think Johnny should have climbed into an attic without light. Either way, he had to get a tetanus shot, and our parents forbade us from coming to play here—which made it more exciting.

"I'll come with you," said Pearl, her smile dimpled.

We ran into the last house inside the boundary, climbed a spiral staircase with no handrail, and went into what would one day be the master bedroom. It smelled like wood chips. There was a skylight cut into the slanted ceiling that let in the evening light. We sat behind a stack of drywall in the middle of the otherwise empty room. The walls were still naked, with pink cotton-candy insulation tucked into the rectangular frames. We leaned back against the drywall, out of breath and sweat beading on our foreheads.

Then we heard Johnny's distant voice. "Ready or not, here I come!"

Pearl looked at me and started to giggle. I tried to keep quiet but soon joined her.

"Shhhh, we'll get caught for sure," I said, but kept laughing.

"It was so boring here last week when you and Ally were gone," said Pearl, tucking stray strands of hair behind her ear.

"I know. I wish we could all have gone away together," I said. "It's going to suck when you're on vacation."

Her family was going camping the next day. Every year our vacations never lined up with Pearl and Johnny's. I thought it would be cool to be twins like them—when they were younger they dressed the same, and they still had one giant birthday party for both of them. Pearl said she would have preferred her own.

Johnny was six minutes older than Pearl, and my best friend, but I thought Pearl got the better name. Mom had told Ally and me about the pearl divers back home who dove deep into the sea, and that a pearl was formed from a speck of sand that gets inside the shell. It irritates the soft flesh until it gets coated with the same material as the inside of the shell. It seemed amazing that such beauty could come from something so accidental.

A playful cry came from someone being found in the house next door; someone would soon come for us, too.

Pearl was looking at me. "Can I tell you something?"

"Sure," I said.

"I wanted to tell you before: I was the one who stole that dirty magazine."

"You did? Why?"

Pearl took a breath and said, "I didn't want you looking at it."

"You didn't want *me* looking at it?"

Pearl shook her head silently. Then she stood and, as if she'd been planning it, undid the top button of her jean shorts.

She pulled the zipper down so slowly, I felt I could hear each tooth separate. Still staring at me, she pulled her shorts and underwear down in one motion. Pearl's privates had just a few strands of hair. Looking at her felt different from looking at the magazine, like she was sharing a secret she hadn't told anyone else.

"Your turn," she said.

I was shy and excited and embarrassed all at once, and more than anything I didn't want Pearl to be standing there alone. I stood up and pulled my shorts down as well. We stood there for I'm not sure how long and explored each other with our eyes.

The last of the sun streamed in from the skylight and specks of sawdust floated in the light. It felt like we were floating as well.

"Olly olly oxen free!" came a voice from the street.

We yanked up our underwear and shorts. Mine got caught on my knees, and I pulled them up too high and gave myself a wedgie. The call came again. But we just stood still. Pearl reached out and touched my hand. My whole body tingled. I leaned in and kissed her. The kiss was short. Our lips barely touched. The second and third time were the same, but during the fourth, I opened my mouth, and so did she. We stopped just as Johnny entered the room.

"Whoa, what are you guys doing?"

"Nothing," we said, jumping away from each other. How hadn't we heard him come up the stairs?

Johnny looked confused. "You two can't kiss."

"It was me who kissed him," Pearl said.

Johnny came over and grabbed her arm. "We're going home!"

"But we just started the game." I put my hands in my pockets, and took them out again. "Who got out first, Johnny?"

"Didn't you hear us calling?" Johnny asked. "Ally got stuck in a basement."

"What! Is she still in there?"

"She's fine. We threw some bales of straw down so she could climb out."

"Okay, good. Those basements, remember when we both got stuck once, Johnny?"

"I don't want to talk to you anymore." Johnny had the same look in his eyes as when he'd stepped on the nail. He turned to Pearl, still holding her arm. "Come on!"

But Pearl broke free. "You're not the boss of me," she said. She stormed past him through the doorway and went stomping down the stairs. Johnny followed her.

I stayed in the room a few moments longer, staring at wood

floor, the stack of drywall, the insulation. It had all happened so fast. But then I remembered Ally and rushed to find her.

"I almost got out on my own," Ally said when she saw me. "I would've if I wore my running shoes."

I didn't ask her if she was okay, instead saying, "I warned you about open basements."

"But it was just such a great hiding spot."

"Still, you could have gotten hurt."

I started walking home and she followed, and asked, "You were hiding with Pearl?"

"Yeah." I wasn't sure if she sensed something. Johnny and Pearl had gone home ahead of everyone else.

The sun was setting and the day was ending. As we walked, I worried Johnny might tell his parents. I don't know what would have happened if he'd come into the room earlier. He used to tease Pearl and me about liking each other when we were younger. We always denied it, and meant it, but things were changing. I couldn't help also being excited by what Pearl and I had shared.

Looking back at the half-built houses, I thought how the future owners wouldn't know how much fun had already happened in them. That the first kiss in their new bedroom wasn't their own. We may not have owned the houses, but during that summer they were ours.

1998

Learn to Care

Vito was the biggest kid in my seventh-grade class. Parker was the smallest. They fought on a spring day after confession. The priest used to come to our school, but he was getting old, so we'd started going to the church instead. Last time, our whole school went for mass and I walked with Ally, but this time only my class went. Between that last time and this time, I wasn't so sure about God anymore.

The air was still damp from a steady morning rain. It had come down hard for a few hours, but nothing like the storm we had last week. I tried not to step on the earthworms that had been forced from their flooded homes and littered the sidewalk. I'd heard that if a worm gets cut in half, both pieces survive and each becomes a whole new worm. Having squashed five worms, Vito picked one up with his bare fingers, ran up behind Parker, and placed it on the shoulder of his yellow raincoat. Then Vito shoved him from behind onto someone's soggy lawn.

"I needed something to confess today," Vito said, and a few boys laughed.

"I'm sure you have plenty already." Parker got up and tried to wipe the mud off his coat with his sleeve, but it just smeared down the front.

"Not as much as you, faggot." Vito had caught Parker with Sarah's bobby pins in his hair last week and had been taunting him ever since.

Miss Allen was swinging up from the back of the line to see what was happening, and Vito quickly slid back into place. Parker stayed on the lawn.

"What happened, Parker?" asked Miss Allen.

"Nothing. I tripped."

"You've gotten your nice coat dirty."

I thought about telling Miss Allen, but I was the second-smallest kid and didn't want Vito picking on me. Our real teacher, Mrs. May, would have found out what had happened and disciplined Vito, but she was off having a baby. Miss Allen was covering for the rest of the year. She believed almost anything we told her. Vito once said he hadn't finished a project because he was out with his mom fundraising for cancer—everyone knew Vito didn't have a mother.

Parker stuck beside Miss Allen for the rest of the walk to the church, where I noticed that the large wooden cross at the front was tilted, hung like an X with one long leg. The storm must have loosened a few bolts. My mom had hung crucifixes outside of Ally's and my bedroom doors. Occasionally, if we slammed the doors, the crucifixes came crashing down. Mom always put them back. Although, last week after we all returned home from the hospital, Dad told us not to do anything to upset her for the next little while, so we closed our doors quietly, pulling them neatly shut.

Our whole class went for confession one by one in the little booth with the soft red curtains. It took forever. I stood in line waiting, wanting to cut myself in two like a worm and be the half that got to wiggle away. I never knew what to say after "Bless me, Father, for I have sinned." Father Baxter should have to confess his sins to me, too; then it would be fair. I told him I stole from my sister and lied to my father. I hadn't stolen anything from Ally, or lied to my father either. With his raspy voice, Father Baxter on the other side of the grating assigned me three Hail Marys. I remember I used to feel good walking out of confession—I think everyone likes to be forgiven. But it felt fake this time—Father couldn't even tell I'd made up my sins.

Father Baxter's face looked tired as he led mass. I could hardly hear his voice when he read from a Letter to the Corinthians. Our class knelt in the two glossy wooden pews at the front. The rest of the church was empty. Two thick candles with crosses printed on them sat on top of the altar. I watched their flames flicker when Father Baxter coughed. It sounded like the type of cough that came with a bad flu, one that might cause something sticky and odd-coloured to be spat up. We waited for him to catch his breath.

Parker sat with his hands together at the end of the front row. He had his eyes closed. There was something about the way he prayed that I both admired and pitied. When we were younger, Ally and I used to pray like that. *Goodnight, God. I'm going to bed with my sleepy head. Thank you for the work and play, thank you for this beautiful day.* We spoke to God like He was in the room with us, and yet when we told Him about our day, we acted as if He hadn't seen it Himself. It had been so much easier to believe then. I never questioned anything about religion—God was a given, and, as Ally used to say, we were "Cat-licks."

When Mom lost her baby last week, my faith flickered like those candles. I couldn't understand why God hadn't done anything to save my second sister. Why He took such a small life before it had even lived. My aunt Audrey came over to our house after it happened and said God wanted the baby for Himself, but that didn't make sense to me. It seemed selfish, considering how much it hurt everyone else. Mom chopped off her own long hair and stayed in bed for a week. I'd never seen her cry like that before. Ally and I joined her and hugged her. It was impossible not to cry, too. I hated the feeling that there was nothing we could do to make it better.

Father Baxter finished coughing and went back to blessing the bread and wine. He moved his hand in the air, making the sign of the cross like he always did, but the action felt silly to me now.

Vito was kneeling one student over from me, directly behind Parker. I watched as he pulled a Bible from the wooden slot. He held it by its spine, reached out, and poked the corners into Parker's hunched back.

Parker's posture straightened immediately, but he managed not to make a sound.

Vito said to the boy beside me, "I think he likes it," and poked him again. Parker turned this time and whispered, "I'm going to tell Miss Allen."

Through a thin smile, Vito mouthed, "I don't care."

I thought of my mother again. *I don't care* was like a swear word in our house. Any time Ally or I said this, Mom immediately gave us a stern look and replied, "*Learn* to care."

Vito's jabs with the Bible continued. Parker slid to the right and leaned as far forward as he could.

I wanted Father Baxter to hurry up so we could go up for communion and Parker would be safe, but Father was taking his time wiping the inside of a gold chalice with a neatly folded white cloth.

Vito, annoyed that he was no longer getting a response, raised the book above Parker's head and brought it down with force; it was a solid hit, making a loud and hollow knock. Parker let out an agonizing "Ahhh!"

Vito quickly returned the Bible to its slot.

Miss Allen came over right away. "We're in *church*," she said to Parker. He was holding his head, but she didn't take any notice.

I wanted to tell Miss Allen what had happened, but I knew if I did, Vito would say I was with Parker, and I'd get knocks to the head, too. I felt sorry for Parker but was afraid to help him.

Father Baxter didn't notice anything either and finally shuffled to the top of the centre aisle with his shiny chalice.

My class stood and filed into a single line to receive communion. Parker's row went first and he held his head where he'd been hit; I had an awful feeling in my chest for staying silent.

With hands folded in front of me, I took a half-step forward in the line every few seconds and stared up at the cross at the front of the church. The longer my eyes were on the cross, the angrier I became—angry at Vito, angry at Miss Allen for not knowing it was Vito, and at Father Baxter for not even noticing. Most of all, I was angry at God for not doing anything again.

I was surprised that I'd reached the front of the line so soon. Father Baxter was holding out the round host. I raised my hands, and he placed it into my palm. The light wafer melted on my tongue, tasteless as always.

When I returned to my seat I put my head down and prayed. I tried to pray from the same place I did when I was younger. After a few moments I knew it wouldn't be the same. So instead, I just told God what I wanted. *Stop Vito from hurting Parker.* I knew we weren't supposed to test God, but He tests us every day. I asked Him to stop it, and if He didn't, I decided right there and then that I'd stop believing in Him. It was a thought that had never come to me before, a thought both satisfying and frightening. I had the power to kill God, by simply not believing.

When we got back to school, it was already lunch hour. As soon as Parker came back outside, Vito went after him. He chased Parker down and cornered him by the portable classrooms. It was like Vito had room in his head for only one idea at a time. Or maybe he was just encouraged by the fact that nothing had stopped him. Most of the other boys gathered around, wanting to see how far he would go. I joined them, wanting to see if God would do anything.

Vito grabbed Parker by his yellow coat and lifted him up against the portable wall so that his feet dangled. Parker squirmed but couldn't get free. Vito was so much taller and heavier that it was hard to believe they were the same age.

Vito punched the space next to Parker's head, rattling the metal wall.

I thought about running and getting help, but someone would see me.

Parker swung his legs, kicking as hard as he could, but Vito held him with both hands and shoved his back against the wall two times.

"Stop," Parker pleaded, tears pooling in his eyes. "That hurts."

"Hey, homo, you think I care?"

Once more, Mom's voice came to me, and I almost blurted out her words.

Vito shoved him again, with even more force than before.

Tears rolled down Parker's face. "It's not fair!" he screamed.

For a second I felt like I might cry, too, but I held it back. God wasn't going do anything. He didn't care, because He didn't exist—if He did, He wouldn't allow such things to happen.

"Vito," I said, surprised by my own voice. "You made him cry.

What more do you want?"

Vito looked at me over his shoulder, gave Parker a last shake, and threw him to the ground. Then he turned to me. "You want to be next?"

Vito's gaze sent a chill through my body. "No," I said, and held my breath. I wanted to turn and run, but stayed standing there.

I heard someone shout, "Principal!"

The other boys scattered, but Vito held his ground.

In those last few moments, I was the only one who saw it all. I saw Parker's clenched jaw and how quickly he was breathing. I saw the rock in his hand and how tightly he gripped it. I saw the fire in his eyes as he raised his arm back. I saw it all, and I stopped believing.

1999

Snapshots

The first snow day of the year was February first. In the front foyer, Ally tried to pull her purple snow pants up high enough to clip on the straps, but the suspenders were tight on her shoulders and the elastic bottoms fit tightly above her ankles. She'd noticed her growth spurt the week before, on her twelfth birthday, when her dad was marking her height behind her bedroom door.

"Let's go, Ally. Johnny's already on the hill," said Aiden. "You're lucky I promised Mom I'd take you with me."

"These don't fit anymore." Ally slid her legs back out and plopped the padded pants on the floor. "I'm just going to go change."

"Okay. I'll go grab the Crazy Carpets from the garage." Ally noticed Aiden's voice had started to sound deeper, like her dad's, and sometimes it slipped into a high, embarrassing squeak.

In her room, Ally tossed the jeans she'd been wearing onto the bed. She took a pair of grey jogging pants out of the dresser and hurried to put them on; it was cold in just her undies. Her hair was still wet against the back of her neck from the shower. Ally liked her showers piping hot. If she could, she would stay in until thick steam covered the mirrors. But she'd been the last one in the family to shower that morning and the water was lukewarm. She came out shivering, goosebumps on her arms and legs.

From the top of her dresser, Ally grabbed the camera her dad had given her. It was the Life Brand disposable one he'd taken to India. There were six pictures left and he'd said she could take them before he developed the roll.

As Ally walked back downstairs, she felt another shiver creep up her back. She put a hand to her forehead but couldn't tell if she had a fever. Her stomach had been hurting the past few days, but she hadn't been able to tell her mom or dad. They'd been busy with doctor appointments, and work, and getting ready for another mouth to feed.

Aiden came back in from the garage with two blue plastic Crazy Carpets.

"Do you know if Pearl is coming?" Ally asked, as she reached the bottom of the stairs.

Aiden said he wasn't sure.

Ally paused at the hallway mirror when she saw her reflection. She rubbed the sleep from her eyes and ran a hand through her hair.

"Trying to look good for Johnny?" Aiden asked.

Ally ran to the door and pointed the camera at him.
Click.

He wrapped a Crazy Carpet around her, tightened the roll, and shook her gently. "You take so long to get ready."

"No, I don't." Ally could only see blue and the ceiling, and it smelled like plastic. She pushed free, put on her coat, and stuffed the camera in the front pocket. It was Aiden's old coat—a boy-coloured blue one that she floated inside. The

186

arms were too long and the coat reached down over her waist. She couldn't wear her purple coat because her wrists stuck out. Her mom had said they'd buy a new one next year but she'd have to make do for the rest of the winter.

The wind was whistling outside as she wiggled her feet into her boots.

"Got everything?" Aiden asked.

"Just need to get my gloves." Rather than taking off her boots, she crawled across the living room carpet to the heating vent where she'd left her gloves to dry. They stood upright with the fingers touching, like two hands in prayer.

She slid her fingers into the toasty gloves and looked up at the framed picture above their couch. The coconut trees and sunny beach seemed so far away, but whenever Ally looked at that picture, a small place inside her felt warm.

Their mom had sat them below the picture last week to tell them she was pregnant again—a surprise this time. It was one year after she'd had a miscarriage, and Ally couldn't help feeling scared her mom might lose this one, too.

"Ally! I'm going," Aiden called.

Ally crawled back and got to her feet just as Aiden opened the front door a crack. A gust of cold air carried snow into the house like a swarm of insects. He shut the door and his excited eyes met hers. She flipped up the hood of her jacket.

Aiden flung open the door. They both rushed outside, and he pulled the door shut behind them.

Beyond Johnny's backyard was a narrow creek at the bottom of a steep valley; on top of the opposite slope was a fence that separated the valley from a field.

The creek had frozen over, so they could slide down either side of the hill carefree. They did a few runs down both sides of the hill before resting at the top by Johnny's backyard. Johnny wore a long blue toque that reminded Ally of the hats the seven dwarfs wore. He would definitely be Dopey with his big ears and rosy cheeks.

"Where's Pearl?" Ally asked Johnny.

"Babysitting," he said, his breath forming clouds in the air, like he was smoking.

"On a snow day?"

"The Bradleys' baby is teething, so she went to help."

"Dad told me he used to dip his finger in a bottle of fenny and rub it on our gums when we were babies," said Aiden.

Ally had heard this, too, but she couldn't remember him doing it. Teeth slicing through gums sounded painful. Maybe it was better to have it happen early.

"What's fenny?" Johnny asked.

"Some kind of alcohol made from cashews."

"Mrs. Bradley would never do that with her baby," Johnny said.

"It works, though," said Aiden.

"And maybe if Mrs. Bradley did," said Ally, "then Pearl could come out and play."

Ally wondered if her dad would use fenny on her new brother or sister's teeth, or if he would have for the sister they'd lost. Afterward, her mom had stayed in bed for a long time. Except for cutting off her long hair, she eventually went almost back to normal. Ally didn't know how she kept going. When she asked, her mom said, "Because we have to. The world keeps turning." Ally was worried it might happen again, but her mom told her all they can do is pray and hope for the best.

"Look, you can barely see our tracks on the hills." Aiden pointed. Snowflakes dotted his red scarf and eyelashes.

"I hope the snow doesn't stop falling," said Johnny. "I want it piled up to here." He made a mark in the air with his hand, well above his toque.

"Think we'll still get many snow days in high school?" Aiden asked.

"I think so. I can't wait."

"You're lucky you don't have to wear a uniform."

"But your school has a better field."

With Aiden, Johnny, and Pearl all going to high school next year, Ally felt left behind. She wanted things to stay the way they were. That's why she liked pictures so much—they didn't change.

She pulled her knees close to her chest and her sled slid away before she could grab it. The sled looked like a raft carried away on a fast-moving river as it skimmed down the hill without a rider. It bounced once on the creek ice and hit the opposite snowbank.

This inspired the boys to build a jump. As they started down the hill, Aiden looked back. "You coming, Ally?"

"I'm going to take some pictures."

They continued down the hill and began to pack snow into a mound where the empty sled had jumped on its own.

Ally pulled out the camera from her coat pocket. She had watched a *National Geographic* program a few days before about a photographer who took pictures of lions in the Serengeti. Ally loved to look through the stacks of old magazines they had in their basement. One of the photographer's lion photos had made the cover of the magazine's latest issue; the photo was of lionesses making a kill, the yellow fur on their faces and the yellow grass around them dark with blood. Ally wondered what it was like to take a bite of a Thomson's gazelle—maybe she'd like the warm, wet taste of raw meat.

She took the glove off her right hand and turned the dial on the camera until a five replaced the six. There was a bird feeder in Johnny's backyard with icicles hanging down the sides. The *National Geographic* photographer had explained that he waits for the moment the earth stands still, then takes the picture. She centred the bird feeder in the camera's viewfinder, but the earth wouldn't stop moving: the wind flared up and snowflakes melted on her bare hand and cheeks. After a few minutes of holding the camera against her face with one eye closed, she gave up.

Click.

Right after she took the picture, she felt a strange feeling in her stomach—not like she was going to throw up, but a deeper pain below her belly button. She sucked in her breath and it went away just as quickly as it came.

Ally was going to go sit down again but she heard Aiden calling her. He stood about three-quarters of the way up the hill with Johnny's saucer-like toboggan in his hands.

"Take one of me going off the jump," he hollered.

She walked down the hill and positioned herself next to the jump.

Aiden sat down and pushed off. He slid down with little speed, yet still got some air off the jump. She tried to take the picture right when he was in the air, but the button wouldn't press down.

"I forgot to turn the dial."

"That's okay. I'll go again."

This time Aiden went from the top of the hill, giving a slight push off again. He held the saucer like a flying carpet in the air.

Click.

"Did you get me?" Aiden asked, before he even came to a stop.

"Got you!"

"Take one of me next." Johnny climbed to the top of the hill. He took a running start, sliding the saucer underneath his knees at the last second, like a coaster under a mug. When he reached the jump, he flew much higher and farther than

Aiden, and the saucer separated from his body mid-air. For a split second it was as if Johnny and the saucer were floating.

Click.

Johnny landed on his butt with a thud. Ally thought for sure he was hurt.

After a few seconds, he looked up and said, "That was awesome!" He collected the saucer and held it out to Ally. "Go try it."

"I don't think I should. My stomach isn't feeling right."

"Come on, Ally, don't be scared. I can take your picture," said Aiden.

"I only have two pictures left." She turned the camera's dial and put it back in her coat pocket.

"Fine," said Aiden.

"Do you know what we should do?" Johnny asked. "Make another jump on the other hill."

"Yeah, and then go down at the same time."

Ally imagined them crashing into one another on the frozen creek—boys were silly sometimes. "Aiden, I'm going to the field to take the last pictures."

"Okay. Just don't go far past the fence."

Ally climbed the other side of the hill and walked to a section of the fence where the ground dipped, and she could crawl underneath. She dug out some snow, lay down flat, and dragged herself below the fence's crisscrossed teeth.

The snow was deeper on the other side. Untouched. With each step, she sank up to her knees. The wind had calmed, and the snowflakes fell larger and more slowly than before. Suddenly hot, Ally unzipped Aiden's old coat. She stuck her tongue out and let a few snowflakes land and melt.

She stopped before a small spruce tree about half her height. Its branches were piled heavy with snow, like each was just about to bend and let its load drop. In the distance, two huge evergreens towered over the field like snow-covered giants. Ally took her camera from her pocket and lay down in front of the sapling. She found all three trees in the viewfinder, with the young evergreen in between the two older ones. She felt like she was inside a snow globe.

Click.

Maybe that would have been the shot the *National Geographic* photographer would take, she thought—if he could have fit under the fence.

Ally tried to turn the dial to take another one, but it stuck between zero and one. End of the roll. She returned the camera to her pocket and lay there for a moment, breathing the winter air.

It was then she felt a warm flow. She sat up on her knees to see a dark bloodstain growing on her jogging pants. The red had stained some of the white snow where she'd been lying. The sight of blood coming from her was terrifying, and she thought at first she might be dying. Then she realized what it was, but couldn't believe it was happening right there and then.

Snowflakes kept falling all around her, but they seemed motionless. It was peaceful yet scary, like she was the only one left on the planet. Ally stayed stuck like this for a little while, but when she felt a shiver, it brought her back to where she was. She zipped Aiden's old coat back up, now thankful that it went down below her waist and hid the stain. She retraced her steps in the snow and crawled back under the fence. She didn't look back.

"Do you want some hot chocolate?" Aiden asked as he closed the front door behind them.

Their mom usually made them a cup whenever they came in from the cold. Ally wished her mom was there now. She thought about calling her but wanted to change her clothes first. "No. I think I'm going to go have a shower to warm up."

Ally kicked off her boots but kept her coat on so Aiden wouldn't see. Instead of putting her gloves on the heater, she tossed them to the floor. Her nose was running as she climbed the stairs to the bathroom, but she was more worried that blood might stain the carpet.

The water from the tap roared. Ally tested it with two fingers first. The water was hot, not just lukewarm, and it stung her fingers, still cold from the outdoors. She undressed and put her stained clothes in a pile beside the scale, unsure of what to do with them. She pulled the lever for the shower and stepped into the tub.

As the steam rose, she saw red in the water at her feet; it swirled and mixed with the falling water before being carried down the drain in a tiny stream. She realized how constant the pain had been only when the shower's heat relieved it. Ally wanted to stay a kid. She wasn't ready to be a woman. Being a woman meant she could have a baby. And lose a baby.

She stayed in the shower until her fingers and toes were wrinkled, and when she got out, the steam had fogged up the room. She dried off with a dark green towel. As she wrapped it around herself, she heard Aiden knock on the door.

"You okay?"

"Yeah," she mumbled. Ally stared at the towels hanging from the closed door and held hers a little tighter. "Can you bring me the phone? I need to call Mom."

Waiting for Aiden to come back, she put the toilet seat down and stepped on top with her bare feet to see out the small window above. She wiped away the condensation; the snow outside had finally stopped falling and everything seemed peaceful again. Eventually she would have to leave the bathroom and return to the world, but she didn't want to yet. As Ally stepped down, she slipped on the closed seat and landed on it with her bum. It hurt everywhere.

When she got up, she tried to look at herself in the mirror, but it was fogged up, too, and she could only see a blurry outline of her body.

Grand Opening

Aiden and I ate kielbasa and crackers in the car while our dad took his time in the mall. I was still upset with him for missing my soccer game, but at least we had a snack. With the windows down and our seat belts off, we took bites from the same coil of kielbasa, doing our best not to get cracker crumbs on the back seat. I wasn't the most careful cracker eater and had to brush crumbs from my summer dress and the blue vinyl seat down to the floor mat.

"Do you know where we're going today?" I asked Aiden.

Aiden took two crackers out of the sleeve. "Down by the bay. Where the watermelons grow."

I continued the song we'd learned at camp a few years ago. "Back to our home, we dare not go, for if we do, our mother would say..."

"Did you ever see a whale, with a peacock tail?" Aiden sang.

"Did you ever see a kangaroo, taking a poo?" I added.

Aiden took a big bite of kielbasa and stuffed in both crackers; they made triangles stick out of his cheeks. I puffed my cheeks up with air and pretended to chew, too. When Aiden saw me, he tried to hold in a laugh but blew bits of dry cracker at the back of my dad's seat.

Days out with Dad were different from days out with Mom. Mom packed lunches and knew where we were going and when we'd be back. Dad seemed to plan as he went, and there'd be big gaps in the day. We'd drive around or see a movie, but he never checked the movie times, so we just watched whatever started soonest. Last time we really wanted to see *The Addams Family*, but it was on later, so we drove around and looked for something else to do in the meantime.

Mom would ask, "How would you kids like to spend your time today?" but Dad said, "We got some time to kill." I wasn't sure sometimes if I should be killing time because there was too much, or spending it like money because there wasn't enough.

Lately, we'd been spending more time with Dad because Mom was a few weeks away from having her baby. I was thinking about putting my hand on my mom's belly and feeling the baby kick, when my dad opened the car door.

"Just me, Ally, sorry. What were you dreaming of?"

"Nothing." I avoided looking him in the eyes. He'd taken a shift at work the day before and missed me scoring two goals to win our soccer team the championship trophy. After the game we got a can of pop, a bag of chips, and a trophy with a tiny gold man, mid-kick, the ball at the end of his foot.

Dad handed us two scratch lottery tickets and reversed the car out of the lot. "See if we're lucky today."

I thought for a moment about not doing the ticket, but I couldn't resist. While Aiden and I scratched away, Dad tapped the steering wheel and hummed along to his Traveling Wilburys tape, our old Chevette clunking when we turned right, the clicker beating extra fast when we turned left. When we were younger, we used to call Dad's car a Corvette, but now we knew the difference. Aiden said we should have got a Pinto to match our last name. I thought so, too.

My lottery ticket was a dud. Aiden won three dollars on his, the cost of another ticket. Mom didn't like Dad buying lottery tickets. He'd won four hundred dollars once, but that was a few years ago. He said his luck had evaporated.

"Where are we going, Dad?" I asked.

"A grand opening." Dad always knew when and where all the new store openings were.

"What kind?" Aiden said.

"The *grandest* kind." He looked in the rear-view mirror to see our reaction, but I looked down at my scratched ticket. I knew Dad wanted to go there because it would likely have free food.

"What about after that?" Aiden asked.

"Depends how much time we have to kill. We could visit Berne in the hospital. We haven't done that yet."

Berne was our old neighbour who had broken her hip coming out of the bath. Mom had said, "How unfortunate for her." Dad said, "Unlucky."

"Or, if you're not up for that, we could go bowling."

Clearly, *Dad* wanted to go bowling. He still had bowling trophies above the fireplace, with the same gold man that topped my soccer trophy, but with the ball on his hand instead of his foot.

"I vote to see Berne," I said, not wanting to do what my dad wanted, even though I didn't really like hospitals. When I was eight, Aiden and I were climbing on Dad's legs while he was watching the hockey game, and I fell off right into the edge of the wall and had to get six stitches. The doctors asked me if my dad had hit me. I told them it was the wall that hit me. As we drove home from the hospital, I heard on the radio the Leafs came back and won the game in the third. Dad clicked his tongue; I could tell he wished he hadn't missed the game, and I remember feeling worse than I had hitting my head.

"Aiden? What do you say?" said Dad.

"I want to go bowling," Aiden said.

"We can go bowling any time," I argued.

"But we haven't been in so long!"

Dad turned the volume of his tape all the way down for a moment and said, "Let's see how this grand opening is first, then decide."

Dad circled the parking lot a few times and finally found a spot, near a sign marked F. We walked toward the crayon-blue building and saw people crowded around the entrance. When I got close enough, I read the yellow letters: IKEA.

Outside the building, a clown with orange hair gave Aiden and me each a yellow balloon and our dad a flyer. We held the strings and punched the balloons at each other.

"Aiden! Enough." My brother was first-born, so he got in trouble first. "You kids need to be sent to boarding school." That was Dad's threat when we misbehaved. He had gone to a school in India run by Jesuit priests; they sounded like robots in robes, swinging their rulers when kids did anything wrong. Most of the priests I knew were more like raisins—plump and shrivelled.

"There are no boarding schools in Canada," Aiden said.

"Then we'll send you to one in India." Dad never put up with us misbehaving in public or fighting with each other—even if it was play. Mom told us, "Your father's family was very strict. They weren't *allowed* to argue. But now, none of them speak to each other. So a little bit of fighting is okay." When Mom had had enough, it was different. She would ask God out loud to send down another barrel of patience for her.

Dad flipped through the flyer. "Look at this—do either of you need a new desk light?"

Aiden came over and looked, and I felt I had to, too.

"Ally, your balloon!" Aiden said.

I must have let go. The balloon floated out of reach, climbing quickly, happy to be free and in a hurry to reach the clouds.

"Ally, you have to be more careful." Dad shook his head. "Now go ask that clown for another one."

"It's okay, Dad, she can have mine," Aiden said.

"Give it here." Dad put the flyer under his arm, took Aiden's balloon, and tied the plastic string tight to my wrist, below my bracelet.

I felt like a little kid with the balloon tied to my arm. I hated how Dad always got mad at accidents. He'd called me an "absent-minded professor" when I left my school bag on the school bus two days in a row. Mom had to call and pick it up both times. She didn't get mad but joked that some brains must have fallen out when I cracked my head. I wondered if lost brains were like lost luck, and balloons that floated away.

The inside of the store was a maze—everything for a home in an organized mess. We walked through the bath, kitchen, and lighting sections before we got to the restaurant, where they were giving away free food to celebrate the store opening. From big cups we drank lingonberry juice, which we were told was Swedish, like the store. Dad ate two hot dogs and Aiden had one, but I still had mine in my hand as we left the restaurant and entered the living room section of the store.

"Dad, I can't finish this," I said.

"Don't waste, Ally. There are starving kids in India who would love that."

"But I'm not hungry."

Dad gave me a look and took the hot dog from me.

Aiden whispered in my ear, "Did you ever see a rhinoceros kissing a hippopotamus?"

I couldn't think of one to say back, and unless I held my arms straight out, my balloon bumped against the side of my head and stuck to my hair. I knocked it away. Everyone else at the store seemed to be having a good time. Some kids were even jumping on the beds.

A man with a short grey beard was coming our way. "Felix!"

"Otis! How ya doing?"

"Good, good. How are things?"

"You know, hanging in there."

"Are these the kids? My goodness. The last time I saw you two, you were below my knees."

"They've grown. They don't eat their food, though." Dad held up my half-eaten hot dog as proof.

The man gave us the same *You shouldn't waste* look my dad did, and I looked away.

"Mine were fussy when they were younger, too," he said. "Now you should see them, they come home and empty the fridge."

He let out a friendly chuckle, like a cartoon bear, and I remembered him—he worked with my dad at the plant.

"Do you kids play any sports?"

"I play soccer," Aiden said.

"Soccer! Excellent."

"I play soccer, too," I piped up. "Left wing."

"That's great, sweetie." The cartoon bear had a broad smile. "I tell ya, she's got her mother's looks. The spitting image. And this guy, he's an athlete."

I didn't like how he only called Aiden an athlete. I scored more goals than him. I liked hearing people say I looked more like my mom, though. Mom joked that the only thing I inherited from my father was his runny nose.

"Dad, can we go try out the couches?" Aiden asked, and I was glad he did—I wanted to get away.

"Okay, but stay in this area. This place is gigantic."

"No kidding," said the man.

"SKRU...VSTA. Not comfortable." My chair was hard and checkered black and white, like a chessboard. "What's yours called?"

"TIRUP. I wonder if it means pear in Swedish?" Aiden's seat was green and shaped like half a hollow green pear.

"Maybe. Let me try it." After Aiden had gotten out, I climbed inside and he started to spin the chair.

I was dizzy when he stopped, and wobbled over to a long sofa with soft red leather cushions, laid my head on the couch's arm, and put my feet up. I stared at the balloon hovering above and waited for my head to stop spinning.

"Little girl." A lady in a uniform came up to me. "Shoes off the sofa, please."

I jumped down, and the balloon yanked against me before floating back up.

"You wouldn't do that at home, would you?"

I didn't say anything back.

The lady shook her head and hurried off. It wasn't fair. Those other kids were jumping on the beds and didn't get in trouble. I just had my feet up because I was dizzy.

I went to a post that had short pencils and paper to write down furniture names. There was a comment box, too. *Did you ever see a sly fox...put a suggestion in a box?* When I folded the paper and dropped it in, the balloon gently bounced off the fire alarm beside the box. Last week someone at school had pulled the fire alarm as a joke. Afterwards, Mrs. Stone asked us each if we did it, but when she came to me, she just said, "You're too innocent to do something like that."

I put the small IKEA pencil in my pocket and went to find Aiden.

"This one is so comfortable. GULLHOLMEN." He sat in a wicker rocking chair shaped like an upside-down cowboy hat. "You okay? Did I spin you too long?"

My eyebrows must have still been squished together because of that stupid lady. I felt the tug of the balloon string around my wrist. "I'm fine." I tried to untie the string. Dad hadn't tied a slipknot, so I couldn't get it. "I'm going to ask Dad to untie this."

"Okay. I'll be here."

I walked back to my dad and the cartoon bear but stopped behind the cabinet when I heard them talking, pulling the balloon into my chest so it wouldn't give me away.

"Did you hear what the union's been saying?" Dad said.

"You know how they are. All we can do is hope for an agreement and no layoffs. And you have another one on the way, too?"

"Yeah, just a few weeks to go."

I'd heard my parents speak about Dad's job before, even though they tried not to talk about it in front of us. When I'd asked them what layoffs were, they were honest. It frightened me at first, but Mom told me, "Only worry about things you can control. The rest, you have to let float up to God to take care of." I wondered if the worries floating up ever collided with the barrels of patience being sent down to Mom.

"Is there any other work you could do?" Dad's friend asked. "What did you do back in India?"

I stayed curled behind the cabinet, clutching the balloon.

"Back home? I almost became a priest, if you can believe. I'd met one too many rotten priests growing up—I wanted to become a good one. But in the end that wasn't a good enough reason. After that, I started working in tool and die. Spent three years as an apprentice, only to become allergic to the paint."

"Unlucky."

"Yeah, I could have been making good money working in tool and die in the Gulf. A friend of mine went to Abu Dhabi and did very well. He lives like a sultan now...and I'm here, struggling to pay the bills. Just think, I might still be a bachelor if I went. I wouldn't have the wife or the kids. Carefree."

My teeth were clenched together. I couldn't listen anymore. I released the balloon and stormed away, that yellow ball trailing along behind me.

Aiden was still lying in the same chair. I went back to the red leather couch and lay down. I didn't care if that lady came back. I would tell her to get lost.

Maybe it would be better if my dad did leave. I tried to picture living with only Mom and Aiden and the new baby, but the balloon was bobbing around and distracting me. I pulled hard at its plastic string, but the knot held. I tried biting it while I pulled, and then grinding it in my teeth, but it still wouldn't break. I hit the balloon and it bounced back.

Dad didn't want us.

IKEA sucked.

Then I remembered the fire alarm.

I walked over to the post and looked around. Nobody was watching. I reached up and pulled the plastic handle. A loud ringing noise blasted through the store and scared me.

I stepped back, not believing what I'd just done. The blaring alarm hurt my ears. I ran and hid behind the red sofa, hugging the balloon. Then, with my heart pounding in my chest, I peeked out above the couch. At first the customers were just looking around, annoyed that their shopping might be interrupted. But then fear spread. People began rushing for the exits, or trying to figure out where the exits were, scrambling past one another and colliding. It was chaos all around.

I crouched down, holding the balloon between my knees, and closing my eyes. I covered my ears and rocked back and forth on my heels—I could still hear the alarm ringing.

When I opened my eyes and peeked back out, there was no one around. And then I heard my father's voice, full of fear.

"Ally! Ally!"

Aiden was calling for me, too: "Ally?"

I spotted them, with the same lady who'd told me not to put my shoes on the couch. She shouted at my dad, "You have to exit the building, sir."

"I'm not going anywhere until I find my daughter. Ally!" he shouted again. Panicked, he looked around corners and behind cabinets. I began to feel guilty. He hurried around the section, frantically pushing chairs out of his way, screaming my name. He tripped on a coffee table and, rubbing his shin, called my name again.

I let go of the balloon and stood.

He looked in my direction and rushed over, picked me up, and squeezed me tight. "You scared me to death. Are you okay, Ally?"

"I'm sorry," I said, tears coming down.

"It's okay, I'm just glad I've found you." He hugged me again. "Now let's get out of here."

Outside, Dad carried me through the crowds of people standing around looking confused. I buried my face in his shoulder, hiding from them all. He didn't put me down until we reached the car with Aiden.

I tried again to untie the string on my balloon. Seeing me struggling, Dad took out his keys, pulled them against the string, and broke it. Then he handed me the freed balloon. I held it for a second and let it go.

"What'd you do that for?"

"I don't want it anymore."

I didn't watch it go. I just pictured the balloon rising up and up, until you couldn't see it at all.

2000

The Elephant in the Mountain

While my parents were getting ready to leave for the funeral home, I held my eight-month-old baby brother, Eric. Ally was playing peekaboo with him over my shoulder.

The person who had died had been my mom and dad's driving instructor when they first came to Canada. Dad was tying his black dress shoes in the foyer and Mom was at the hallway mirror putting cream on her face. "Remember the O'Briens are home next door," she said, "and the emergency numbers are on the fridge." Mom always worried about emergencies. She kept baking soda next to the stove and had so many flashlights in the house that Ally and I prayed for a blackout so we could use them for once.

"We should get going," Dad said to Mom, putting on his suit jacket.

Mom put on her jacket as well and said, "Aiden, try to get him to finish both jars of food in the fridge."

"I will. I've fed him so many times with you here, Mom."

Mom said she knew, gave each of us a kiss, and followed Dad out the door. Halfway out, she turned and said, "And don't answer the door if it's not someone you know." Then she closed the door and locked it from the outside.

Before Eric, when she and Dad left us home alone, Mom used to say, "If a stranger comes, just tell them, 'My mom's in the shower.'" But then one time, a couple carrying Bibles came to the door. When the man asked if our mother was home, Ally said, "She's in the shower." The woman asked if our father was available. Ally had been surprised by this question and glanced over at me. I panicked and said, "He's in the shower, too." The man and woman eyed each other and said they'd come back.

Almost as soon as our parents were gone, Eric started crying.

Ally gently tickled his feet. He smiled and squealed, and we went to work getting him ready for his bedtime.

The last of the evening sun lit my parents' bedroom, bouncing off their mirror and sending a little rainbow to the foot of the crib.

Eric wouldn't fall asleep. He kept crying, mouth open, eyes shut.

"Eric, what's wrong?" Ally put her hand in the crib and let him grab her pinky finger.

I lifted him out of the crib, his tiny hand still holding Ally's finger tightly.

"Did you burp him?" Ally asked.

"Yeah. He spat up a bit." I showed her the stain on my T-shirt near the collar: a mix of peas and strawberry baby food. When I'd tried to feed him, he spit the peas out with a look of disgust, so I had to slip them in between spoonfuls of strawberry. That way I got him to finish both jars, just as Mom had said.

"You changed him?" I asked.

"Right before you fed him." Ally undid the diaper sticker and peeked. "Nothing."

I leaned in and sniffed, but only smelled the coconut oil Mom used on his skin.

Ally ran her fingers through his soft, black hair. The cries kept coming. I carried him over to the rocking chair next to my parents' bed, then rocked the chair back and forth, but Eric kept crying.

"Should we call Mrs. O'Brien?" Ally asked.

"If we do that, Mom and Dad won't ever leave us home alone with him again," I said.

"Maybe he's sick again."

Eric had caught a cold a few weeks back. He had a mini-cough, and when his nose got stuffed up, Mom had to suck the snot out from his nostrils and then spit it out. It was the grossest thing I'd ever seen. "What else can you do?" Mom said. "You can hold a tissue up to a baby's nose, but telling a baby to blow isn't going to work. I did the same for both of you when you were babies, because I love you." I changed Eric's diapers, gave him baths, and burped him, but I didn't think I could suck his snot into my mouth.

"I don't think so," I said, feeling Eric's forehead. "Maybe he just needs a story." I thought back to the ones Mom used to tell us before we went to bed. "How about 'The Elephant in the Mountain'?"

"Can I tell it to him?" Ally sat on the bed next to the rocking chair.

I nodded. Eric's body was tense against my chest, and I was getting worried. His arms and legs kept squirming and his cries started to hurt my ears.

"Once upon a time," Ally began, "in a faraway land, there lived a herd of elephants. And because the elephants had five toes instead of four, they were Asian elephants. So, the faraway land had to be somewhere in Asia."

"Ally, that's not part of the story."

"Mom always adds things to her stories. I'll get all the important stuff in."

"Fine, keep going," I said. Eric still had tears in his eyes, but his cries were a little less piercing.

"In this faraway land in Asia, a new elephant had been born. A very special elephant. His name was Om, and he was born on the day the sun hid behind the moon. The elder elephants had said it was a day of great fortune, but they changed their minds later when they realized something about the new elephant. Om tripped over the ground much more than any other young elephant. Although he always tried to keep his trunk in contact with his mother, Radha, he kept running into her legs. If Om ever lost contact with Radha, he'd wander and accidentally get knocked over by the other elephants.

"'An elephant that can't see won't survive,' the elder elephants said to Radha.

"'He will, as long as I love him,' Radha said.

"And so Radha only let Om walk underneath her, to protect him. Om learned to walk within her four legs until he could walk behind his mother, holding her tail with his trunk. The only place where Radha didn't have to guide Om was in the water. The large pond was Om's favourite place. He was clumsy everywhere else, but in the water he could feel all around himself and swam easily. Om could spend all day there—he loved to shoot water from his trunk as high up in the air as he could, then feel it sprinkle down onto him.

"But Om's happiness didn't last long. It had not rained in a very long time, and each day the large pond shrunk a little bit. Eventually the water turned muddy. At different times during the day, many other animals, from the deer to the monkeys, huddled around the edge to drink. Even the tiger, who kept to himself most times, came out to sip the water.

Radha noticed the way the tiger eyed Om, and she made sure when he came to the pond there were other elephants around.

"The elder elephants told the herd it was time to move on, to cross the dry lands to find water. Radha pleaded with the elders, 'But Om won't survive such a long journey.' The elders said, 'But if we stay, we'll run out of water.'

"Radha didn't know what to do. If she stayed, they'd run out of water, and she'd have to keep Om safe from the tiger on her own."

Ally paused the story to glance at Eric. His cries had quieted. With the chair rocking back and forth, he was calm against my shoulder, and I was calm, too.

"But don't worry, Eric," Ally continued, "that's not how the story ends. It wouldn't be a very good bedtime story if it did. Luckily, one of the birds, a little golden oriole that sometimes rested on the elephants' heads, had overheard Radha. The golden oriole said, 'I know where you can find water, but it's in the mountain and only the birds who can fly visit it. All others who go in never come out.'

"'Please take us there,' Radha said.

"And so, before the other elephants left, the three of them headed for the mountain, with the golden oriole perched on Radha's head and Om holding on to Radha's tail. Soon they were climbing the mountain's slope, but they had to stop often so Om could keep up.

"The oriole stopped them once along the way at a deep hole in the thick stone, a hole as wide as Radha. 'The water is down there.'

"'But how do we get to it?' Radha said, carefully looking far down below.

"'We have to go to the other side.'

"And so they pressed on to the other side of the mountain.

213

Radha soon let Om walk ahead and held her trunk under him, lifting his body to lighten his walk.

"When they finally reached the other side, they were all very tired, but when they saw the cave, they perked up. They entered the cave, and it became narrower and narrower the farther they walked. There was an opening up ahead, but Radha realized it was too small and she couldn't take Om any farther.

"The oriole flew ahead into the opening of the cavern and then returned.

"'Is the water through that opening?' Radha asked.

"'Yes, but if he goes down there, he won't be able to get back out. The walls are smooth and run straight down. But there is an island in the middle that's shaped like an egg and big enough for him to stay on. There are plants and trees and bugs, and light comes in through the hole we saw.'

"Om did not want to leave his mother. It was difficult for Radha as well, knowing she was sending Om somewhere she could not follow. But she told him, 'My love will keep you alive.'

"Om walked farther into the cave and was just small enough to squeeze through the opening.

"Radha heard a splash a few seconds later and got worried, but when she heard laughter and saw water trickling from the hole, she knew he was okay.

"That day Om sprayed so much water up into the air, the mist rose from the hole, and a rainbow formed over the mountain.

"Radha visited him as often as she could and gathered fruit to drop down the hole.

"The golden oriole told the other birds about the elephant in the mountain, and the birds told the monkeys and other animals. Whenever they passed by the hole, they would also try to drop some fruit down.

"As time passed, a stream of water flowed out from the cave. This stream grew stronger as the years passed, and ran down the mountain even in the driest days when there was no rain. All the animals drank and drank and thanked the elephant."

Ally stopped the story. With her hand against her tilted head, she indicated that Eric was asleep.

Before my parents came home, I laid Eric back in his crib and thought of him dreaming of the elephants, like Ally and I had when we were younger. I pictured the elephant in the mountain then and thought again about what had kept him alive.

1996

Hold It Like a Butterfly

When I was nine years old, I received a love letter from the son of the man who came to build our deck. While I no longer have the letter, I remember those few days as clearly as I remember any from my childhood.

The deck wasn't very large, but it was a big deal to my family all the same. We'd lived in that red-brick house for years, and my parents hadn't done anything to it, not even paint. The walls were still builders' white. Dad used to say that the house belonged to the Royal Bank of Canada. I worried that a banker in a dark suit might come knocking on our door and force us to leave at a moment's notice. So getting a deck built in the backyard finally seemed to be a sign that the house was ours. I knew the deck was mostly for Mom, though. She often told me and Aiden how she missed sitting outside in the mornings to have a cup of tea, like she had back in Goa.

I was trying to grow my hair out that summer and wore it in pigtails tied with red elastics. Grade 3 had finished a few weeks earlier, and Aiden had gone to a friend's cottage. Only Mom and I were home when the men dropped off a stack of lumber almost as tall as me in the backyard. It sat next to our maple tree, the only tree I preferred to sit under rather than climb. My favourite spot was between two exposed roots that formed the arms of a little chair with the trunk as its back.

The builder was supposed to come at ten that morning. Dad had found the guy through someone at work. He said he was Indian, but not Indian from India, like us.

At half past ten, Mom worried about the directions she had given him, and tried to call but got no answer. By eleven-thirty, she gave up and said she was going to start on her essay. Mom had been a teacher in India but was having to do her education over again to be one here.

Out the front window, I saw a white van pull up and I called Mom over.

A man wearing a faded red baseball cap, blue jeans, and a tool belt stepped out of the van. When he opened the sliding door, it fell right off the van onto our lawn.

"Oh, brother," Mom said.

The man picked up the door with both hands and reattached it.

We moved away from the window so he wouldn't catch us spying on him. But Mom opened the front door before he knocked, so he must have known. I stood next to my mom and was surprised to see a boy standing next to the man. He was a little taller than me and his black hair was longer than mine.

"Hi there—Clarissa, right?" said the man.

"Yes, Jim. I spoke to you on the phone."

They shook hands.

"Sorry I'm late, had to pick up my boy. He was supposed to go with his mother..." Jim paused. "Anyway, he'll be here the next few days with me. Hope that's okay?"

"Oh, no problem." Mom turned to the boy. "What's your name?"

The boy held a coiled notebook at his side and looked up for just a moment before his eyes returned to the floor. "Joseph."

"Joseph and Jim. I'm going to get those mixed up, you watch," Mom said. "Are you going to help your dad, Joseph?"

He shook his head, embarrassed, then glanced at me for a second and looked away.

Jim patted his boy's shoulder. "He doesn't take after his father."

They weren't dressed like the Indians on TV, or the ones I'd learned about on a class trip to Crawford Lake that year. Everyone on that trip got a dream catcher with netting like a spider's web and feathers hanging below. I hung it in my bedroom window to make sure only good dreams would come to me. Mom said she was glad I went there and told me Canada is rightfully their land and that it was stolen years ago. I tried to imagine all of Canada being stolen, but all I could picture was that same banker in a dark suit forcing people from their homes.

"Did they bring the wood already?" Jim asked.

"Yes, early this morning. Come, let's go to the backyard." Mom slipped on her sandals and led Jim and his son out the front door and around the house. My flip-flops were at the back door, so I went through our house instead.

In the kitchen, I stood on my tiptoes and peeked out the window above the sink. While Mom showed Jim the bamboo-stick outline she'd made where the deck would go, Joseph went over to the maple tree and sat down—right in *my* spot. He looked up and met my eyes through the window, forcing me to crouch by the cabinets.

But it was silly to be hiding in my own house. I took a carton of chocolate milk from the fridge and filled a tall glass from the cabinet. Aiden and I always argued over which glass held more—the tall skinny ones or the short fat ones. It was important to know which glass was the biggest for when we had guests over and were allowed to drink pop.

When I turned around, Joseph was at the window looking in. I nearly jumped, and felt the drink slip from my hand. The glass shattered on the tile, and creamy brown milk splattered on the floor and cupboards.

"Crap!" I put my hand over my mouth as soon as I said it, then looked back out the window, but Joseph was gone.

Mom came in a few moments later. "Stay put, Ally." She kept her sandals on and gathered the bigger broken pieces into what was left of the base of the glass, then put them into a plastic milk bag. We agreed I was lucky my dad wasn't home—he always got angry with Aiden and me if we broke something, saying we needed to be more careful. Mom got my flip-flops and I helped her sop up the chocolate milk with paper towels and sweep up the shards of glass that had scattered all the way to the corners of the kitchen.

When we finished cleaning up, I looked out the window again. Joseph was back in my spot under the tree.

That afternoon, Mom stood next to the sink with a cutting board. She used a long knife to remove white globs of fat and goosebumped skin from chicken legs and thighs. Everything she sliced away from the chicken was pushed off the cutting board into the sink. She gave the milky pink pieces of meat a quick rinse under the tap before placing them in a metal bowl. I didn't like raw chicken—it was one step too close to the chicken being killed.

"What are we having for dinner?"

"Chicken curry."

"Can't we just have barbecue?"

"Not tonight, honey. I've got to finish this before your father comes home and then get to work on my essay before my shift tonight."

"Can I have Kraft Dinner, then?"

Mom stopped cutting and looked out the window. "Ally, can you do me a favour? Go ask Jim and his son if they need water. It must be hot out there in the sun."

I hoped she wouldn't also ask me to bring a jug of water out. I might drop that, too.

When I got outside I was surprised at how much had been done in just a few hours. The lumber lay in stacks around the yard, with a workbench and the tools in the centre. There were two deep, round holes in the grass, and next to the holes sat a large pile of fresh dirt with a shovel stuck in it. I didn't see Joseph by my maple tree, but Jim was behind the pile of dirt—he was bent over, drinking from the garden hose. It wasn't until he stood up straight and wiped his mouth with the back of his hand that he noticed me.

"Hello there." He had a crooked front tooth, but his smile was too wide for him not to seem like a nice person. "Do you want a drink?" He held up the hose, water flowing out.

I took the hose and held it sideways, like eating corn on the cob. I'd learned to drink this way because Aiden always kinked it to try to spray the water in my face.

"Can you do me a favour, young lady?" Jim picked a few tools out of a nearby white plastic pail. "Can you fill this guy up to here?" He took the pencil from behind his ear and made a mark on the inside of the bucket. The pencil looked like it was sharpened with a knife, into a rough pyramid instead of a cone.

"Sure." I directed the water into the pail, going from a hollow splat noise to a pee-into-toilet sound.

"Thanks. I'm just going to grab the concrete from the van."

Jim walked around the side of the house. The water reached the mark he'd made, and I pulled the hose over to Mom's garden and laid it down. I looked over at the maple tree and noticed Joseph's notebook in my spot, like he'd left it there for me. I went over and opened it. Out rolled a blue pencil sharpened the same way as Jim's, and on the inside cover he'd written *Joseph Billy*. It turned out to be a sketchbook, not a notebook. There were birds, rivers, and trees drawn in detail and shaded in a way that made it seem like they were moving.

"That's mine!" Joseph grabbed the notebook from me. There was a small scar above his left eye that I hadn't noticed before.

"Sorry."

"Who said you could look at it?" He took a step toward me and my body went tight.

"Joseph." Jim returned carrying a bag of concrete on his shoulder and dropped it next to the pail with a thud. "Why don't you go turn off the water, son."

Joseph obediently went to the side of the house where the faucet was.

"Don't mind him, sweetie," said Jim. "He's been in an awful mood all morning. Just leave him be for now."

The water from the hose trickled to a stop. Jim opened the bag of concrete, approved how much water I'd put in the bucket, and poured the concrete in. A small cloud of dust rose into the air and made me sneeze.

"That's a mighty big sneeze for such a small person," he said, in a way that sounded like a compliment.

Jim attached a contraption to his drill that looked like a silver coat hanger bent into a long J. He dipped it into the pail and turned on the drill. The metal attachment spun, mixing the water and concrete. It reminded me of the hand blender Mom used to mix wet and dry ingredients for her pineapple-and-coconut cake. Afterwards, she would give Aiden and me each one of the metal beaters to lick clean.

I watched Jim pour the concrete into one of the holes in the ground, but went inside when Joseph came back. I was scared of him. The rest of the day I only peeked out the window once: he was sitting under the tree in my spot again.

The next morning, the whine of an electric saw startled me awake. Jim and Joseph had returned.

After a strawberry Pop-Tart breakfast, I avoided the backyard and went across the street to call on my friends, Johnny and Pearl, but they were still away at their grandma's. Mom was in her room working on her essay so I watched *The Price Is Right*. The contestant was wearing a *Don't Mess with Texas* T-shirt. He didn't listen to the audience shouting and overpriced his bid.

When I heard Mom in the kitchen I went to meet her. "Are you finished your essay?"

"Just a quick break." She held a hefty mango in her hand, brought it to her nose, and said, "This is a good one." Dad joked sometimes that she must have been a fruit fly in another life.

Mom glanced out the back window as she took out two plates and a knife. "Ally, why don't you go outside? It's so nice out. You should go play with Joseph, he's probably bored."

"It's too hot. I was going to read inside."

Mom held the knife over the mango like she was about to cut a birthday cake, then sliced along the seed. The flesh was bright orange. She'd given a mango to Pearl's mom once but didn't tell her how to cut it. Pearl told me her mom spent a few minutes trying to saw right through the seed before she gave up and threw it out.

Mom cut four large chunks of mango onto one plate, leaving the skin on. I got the seed, a slippery, tricky treat. I loved to scrape the juicy flesh from the seed with my front teeth and afterwards pick out the fibres stuck between them.

Mom ate two pieces, then gave me the plate. "Why don't you go offer these to Jim and his son. Looks like they're having

225

lunch." Before I could respond, she added, "Back to my essay," and went upstairs.

My first thought was to just eat the remaining pieces, but Mom's desk upstairs overlooked the backyard and she would know if I didn't go.

I rinsed my hands under the tap for longer than normal. I was nervous about facing Joseph again and thought he might try to fight me. I went to the family room and, from the glass jar on the mantel that had my seashells, I found the one Dad had given me. It stood beside his old slingshot that we weren't allowed to use, though he promised he'd teach us one day. Dad had brought the slingshot and the shell with him when he first came to Canada. When he gave me the shell he said it was from Baga Beach, near his old home. He told me he wanted to bring part of the ocean with him. I hadn't seen the ocean yet—the closest thing we had nearby was a lake that we couldn't swim in. I put the shell in my pocket and went outside with the plate.

I could smell the sawdust and wood chips that littered the grass. The deck was beginning to take shape; I was careful to step over the frame as I carried the mango out. Jim and Joseph were sitting on a stack of lumber.

"My mom asked me to check if you wanted some mango."

"Sure," Jim said. "But only if you take some cheese in exchange." He held out a Babybel wrapped in red wax.

I agreed, and they each took a slice of mango from the plate. I peeled the wax from the cheese and ate it in three bites. Then I rolled the wax into a ball, took out my shell, and pressed the wax onto its outside.

"Delicious. Thank you, Ally." Jim placed the mango skin back on the plate.

I looked at Joseph to see if he was done but didn't see his mango skin. He had an embarrassed look on his face and said, "I didn't know you weren't supposed to eat the skin."

"It's okay," I said. "Some people eat the skin, too."

"What's that you have in your hand?" Jim asked me.

"It's a shell my dad gave me. If you put it to your ear you can hear the ocean. A girl in my class said it's only your blood moving that makes the noise, but I don't think so."

"Can I see, please?" Joseph said. I was surprised he asked so nicely, and when he took the shell I felt the roughness of his fingertips on the palm of my hand for just a second.

"Back to work for me." Jim packed up his lunch and returned to measuring lengths of wood around the frame.

Joseph held the shell up to one ear, then the other. "I hear it, but what's that other water sound?"

"Oh, that's our next-door neighbour's pond. Mr. Fanning. There used to be fish in the pond but the racoons ate them—he swore so much that morning. He's kind of mean. When our tennis balls go over his fence, he doesn't let us go get them." I paused. "Do you hear the wind chimes?"

Joseph nodded.

"Those are Mrs. Gardner's. Our neighbour on the other side. She's nicer."

"Do you hear that whistling?" he asked. "That's my dad."

Joseph had one crooked tooth like his dad, and an even wider smile.

Jim was whistling a song I recognized but couldn't remember the words to. His hammering seemed to keep time with the tune. He was so quick, as if the hammer were a part of his arm. Two taps to hold the nail in place and two harder ones to drive it clean into the wood.

Joseph and I listened as the hammer and whistle blended with the other backyard sounds. Then I realized we were both just standing there, and I got nervous and started to talk again.

"Mrs. Gardner gave us that honeysuckle plant over there. Do you want to try one?"

I picked the thin flower and sucked the sweet drop of nectar from its base.

Joseph handed back my shell and did the same with another flower.

I felt a sneeze coming on again. My head tilted back, but I put my finger under my nose, like a moustache, and stopped it.

Just then Joseph let out a big "Ha-choo!" It was as if he'd stolen my sneeze. We looked at each other and laughed.

A monarch butterfly landed on one of the honeysuckle flowers. Joseph slowly brought both hands up and around the monarch. I thought he was going to kill it, until I saw how delicately he held its orange, black, and white spotted wings.

"If you hold them too tight you'll crush them. Too loose and they'll fly away."

He brought the butterfly to his mouth and started whispering. He lowered it, and then held it up to my face. "Make a wish."

"Why?"

"Just whisper a wish, and it'll come true. Butterflies can't make any sound. They can't tell anyone your secret. It's true, my mom told me."

Joseph seemed really proud of this, so I leaned in. I couldn't think of a good wish so I asked for a million more wishes in a whisper too quiet for him to hear. Joseph whispered as well but took longer to make his wish—I had a feeling it was for something real. He let the butterfly go, and it fluttered away.

On the third day, the sound of hammering woke me with less of a scare. I had dreamt of the ocean. I was a fish, swimming with many others. When I tried to swim free, going whichever way I wanted, I got separated from the school. I wandered the ocean, trying to find those like me, except I woke up before I found anyone. My dream catcher must not have been working.

I wondered if Joseph believed in them, after what he'd shared about butterflies.

That morning, I had to go grocery shopping with Mom. By the time we got back and put everything away, it was afternoon.

The deck looked like a deck now, yet my first steps onto it were cautious.

"Almost done," Jim said to me from the other side, where he was working on the stairs. "It's safe. Go on, jump as hard as you can."

I did a little hop first, but when I felt how sturdy it was, I jumped twice, full strength.

"Attagirl." He stood up and turned to Joseph, who was sitting on the grass next to the toolbox and a loose pile of wood. "Just gotta run to the hardware store. I'll be back in a flash."

Joseph nodded. I walked over and sat beside him on the grass. He had a magnifying glass in his hand and directed the sun to a point on the rubber sole of his shoe. I saw no smoke, yet there was a funky smell in the air.

He reached over to the pile of wood and pulled a long piece in front of him. Raising the magnifying glass, he started to burn dark lines into the light wood grain with the sun's rays. I stayed quiet as he drew. A shape started to appear—a shell. And beside it, the outline of a butterfly.

When he finished, all I could do was stare. I'd never been given a gift like that. I didn't know what to say, and so I said the first thing I could think of: "I'm thirsty."

"I'll go turn on the water." Joseph ran to the side of the house.

The hose, coiled in the grass like a snake, came alive. I held it and drank.

Joseph came back and I handed him the hose. He held it vertically like his father. I couldn't resist bending the hose into a kink. He leaned in and looked right into the spout just as I let my grip loosen. Water gushed into his face. He covered his eye with both hands. I moved closer to see if he was okay, but caught the smile forming in his cheeks too late. He put his thumb to the spout and sprayed me from head to toe. I let out a scream and tried to wrestle the hose away from him. Our laughter joined the other backyard noises as water flew in all directions.

Jim finished the stairs that afternoon. "Let your mom know there's just the railing to do tomorrow," he told me. "Should only take a couple hours."

As Jim packed up for the day, I realized we hadn't saved the piece of wood with the burned-in drawing. I told Joseph, and he said he'd help me find it tomorrow. I wanted to give him a hug goodbye but thought his dad or my mom might see me and I chickened out. Instead, I waved goodbye to him, even though I was right beside him. He waved back, and I went inside. Everything seemed darker as my eyes adjusted. It reminded me of coming out of a movie theatre during the day—your eyes go from dark to light instead, but it was the same feeling. Sometimes, if the movie is really good, you're not ready to go back to the world you knew.

I got excited the next morning when I heard the hammering from the backyard. It was the last day Joseph would be coming, and I wanted it to be special. I braided my hair and put on my favourite pair of jean shorts. Mom never wore perfume—I looked for some in her room but didn't find any. I settled for a perfume sample in an old copy of *Chatelaine* that Pearl had given me. I rubbed the page on my neck, and from my shell collection I picked out one I'd found at Sauble Beach to give to Joseph. It was shaped like a mini ice cream cone with a hole at the top.

When I went outside, Jim was putting up the railing, but I didn't see Joseph anywhere.

"Where's Joseph?" I asked.

"Oh, his mother came and took him."

I waited for Jim to say more, but he directed his attention back to his work.

Back inside, I kept pressing the shell's point into my thumb as I looked out into the backyard. My spot under the maple tree was empty. I went to put the shell back in the glass jar, but instead took my dad's slingshot, put the shell in, and fired it against our couch. It just bounced off the floral orange cushions. I put the slingshot back so I wouldn't get caught.

Jim completed the railing in an hour. Mom finished her essay that morning, too. She told Jim he'd done an excellent job and wrote him a cheque.

As he folded the cheque and slid it into his pocket, I asked, "We need painting done, too, can you do it?"

Jim said he did paint, too. Mom told him we might be in touch, and he thanked her again, then packed up the last of his tools and drove away.

Mom took a couple of weeks to call Jim, and when she did, the number was disconnected. It was a scary feeling to realize how easily people can enter and exit our lives.

When I found Joseph's message at the end of the summer, I was practising with the slingshot. Dad had finally taught me how to use it. I had to use a rubber ball and shoot away from the house, but I was getting good at knocking empty cans off the railing. After hitting two of the three cans I'd set up, I went to fetch them and noticed something on the underside of the railing. It was the drawing Joseph had made with the magnifying glass. There was a shell, a butterfly, and a heart in between. My first love letter, written with the sun, now hidden in a place the sun couldn't reach.

We moved from that house a few years later. By then, Mom had found a teaching job. The banker forcing us from our house never materialized, and yet we still left sooner than any of us expected. Mom got pregnant with my baby brother, Eric, and our house became too small.

My maple tree lost its leaves early the year we moved. Dad said, "It knows we're leaving." He told me that the year he moved to Canada, a mango tree on the family property stopped giving fruit. All life left the tree and it stood like a stone for years before it was eventually brought down by the monsoon rains.

I made sure to say goodbye to my tree before we left. I sat in my spot and held my hand against its roots for a long while. I wished we could have taken it with us. I'd wanted to take the section of deck railing where Joseph's drawing was, too, but that meant I would have had to tell someone else it was there. I'd gotten a camera for my previous birthday and later I couldn't believe I didn't think to take a picture of it before we moved. When I looked at it that last time, like every time before, I wondered where Joseph was. I remember learning that summer just how delicate love could be.

Our neighbourhood friends, Pearl and Johnny, had told us that after we left, the people who moved into our house changed everything. They ripped up the deck and put in a stone patio. Even though it was their house, I resented them for it. That feeling faded as our new house became our new home. Somewhere between house and home, I grew up. I went to high school. And after high school I left for college in Toronto.

The autumn air is cool as I walk toward OCAD for my photographic history class. I hold a warm tea in my hands and pass students on the sidewalk wearing scarves and jogging pants with *U of T* printed in white on their bums.

I'm early and take my time to admire Beverley Street's deep

yellow-and-crimson foliage, and the large houses of weathered brick. My apartment is in the basement of one such house farther north on St. George. I'm lucky to have an apartment to myself, but the couple upstairs get into intense shouting matches and sing together when they make up. I put on headphones or go for a walk. Since I moved in September, I haven't ventured too far or often outside my neighbourhood, and when I do, I draw little maps on crumpled pieces of paper so I don't get lost. The city still feels huge compared to home.

Before I reach Grange Park, I stop at a wooden telephone pole. There are layers of posters stapled to it—the top one is for a show by a band named Wine Jacket. The wood looks scarred by the staples driven on top of each other, rusted and black. I place my tea on the concrete next to my sneakers while I take the cap off my camera and snap a photo.

I find a bench in the park and sit and sip my tea. Mom's habit of sitting outside with a cup of tea has made its way to me. If only her culinary skills had as well. Mom packs me a couple of small containers of chicken curry to take home when I visit, which I usually end up eating my first day back at school. When Mom calls, she asks what I've eaten, while Eric and Dad ask when I'm coming home next. Each time I go home for a visit, I tell myself I make the journey for my parents' and brother's benefit, but, honestly, I miss the chaos, the jokes, the fights, and the closeness that only those called family share. I'd made a few friends in class, and love the variety of people and anonymity the city provides, and yet I still feel lonely walking back to my place.

I drink the last gulp of tea, sweeter than the rest, and pull out Aiden's postcard from India. He addressed it to *Ally-cat* and drew a small claw beside it. I laugh again when I read, *Despite my life being dictated by bowel movements, the food is unreal.* He talks about our family there, and how there are *So. Many. People.* He asks how everything's going on my end and signs it with love, and, *P.S. Ally, this place changes everything. You have to come.* After I finish school, I will.

I notice a black squirrel nearby vigorously digging a hole in the grass. He moves a few yards over and starts to dig again. I wonder how many trees grow from the nuts that squirrels bury and forget about.

A larger grey squirrel approaches the first one and a chase begins. I follow their zigzags with my eyes until they both dart up a tree to my right. Then I notice the maple tree next to the one they ran up. Well, not so much the tree, but the young man sitting against its trunk. He has long dark hair and his bare knees stick through two frayed holes in his faded black jeans. The way he's hunched over his notebook looks oddly familiar. I tell myself it's likely someone else, but a feeling in my stomach urges me to investigate.

I walk to a garbage bin that's beyond where he sits, but don't pass by close enough to catch a glimpse of his face. I toss my cup in the garbage and loop back, this time coming straight up behind him.

As I approach him, my steps are careful. My heart pounding.

I'm close enough to see over his shoulder now; what I see on the page is the city coming alive as I've never seen it before. His hands look dry, and his left holds a pencil that makes quick and crisp lines blending into gentle shades. The scene looks like a dream. Or maybe a memory.

Then I notice the point of the pencil in his hand—the edges and tip are flat, like they were sharpened with a knife.

2006

Coconut Dreams

Four days in Goa nearly killed me. It started the morning my bus arrived in Mapusa and I couldn't find my uncle Quinton. A swarm of rickshaw drivers crowded me as I tried to dig my bag from the cavity of the bus. "My uncle is picking me up," I repeated, heaving my backpack onto my shoulders. Less than a week before Christmas, the morning sun was scorching. I pulled my cell phone from my backpack—one bar of battery power—and found my uncle's number.

When he answered, there was a dog barking in the background, and I struggled to hear him at first.

"Aiden. Where are you?" Uncle Quinton's soft voice reminded me of the voice of his daughter, Maria, the cousin I'd just left in Mumbai the night before.

When I told him I'd reached Mapusa he was surprised. "So soon?"

"The bus was early," I said. "I only have one bar of battery left."

"You're at the bar?"

"No, no. My phone. It's low on battery. I'm...next to the road, in front of a market."

He told me to stay put and he'd come.

While I waited I looked at the market. Bright oranges, yellows, and pinks shone amid the dust. A light breeze carrying sweet and sour scents wove through stalls of bangles, electronics, and clothing, and women in saris sat on straw mats piled with fruit: bananas, guavas, pomegranates, and papayas as big as watermelons. A very old woman squatted beside a woven basket full of fish that looked like the minnows we used to catch in the creek back home. They were the same size and shape, but the morning sun lit their skin like silver coins. The fish glistened despite a small horde of flies, which dodged the fishmonger's flapping, wrinkled hand.

Voices spoke in Konkani, but I had only learned a few swear words. On the overnight bus, they had made the stop announcements in Hindi. Maria and her mother had warned me when I left Mumbai to be careful on the bus. Maria's mother said, "Listen for the name of the city. And remember your bus number if you get off at a rest stop. They all look the same, and sometimes these drivers leave quick, and you will be stuck." I only got off the bus once at night. I followed a line of men into a concrete bunker where the urinal was just a metal wall and a drain in the floor. Heat came off the metal like a radiator.

The line for food was even longer. I was thankful my aunt Delilah, whom I'd met again in Mumbai after many years, had packed me cutlets in a foil package for the journey. "These places the drivers get paid to stop at, more oil than food you get," she said. I ate in my seat and looked out the window at the night sky. I'd heard Venus and Jupiter would be visible, but I didn't expect to see them above a crescent moon, making a smile in the night sky. I hoped the celestial sign meant I was headed in the right direction. Leaving university without a degree had left me uncertain of everything.

"Canada, you want to buy a bracelet?" A boy held a sheet of cardboard with lines of woven string bracelets attached. He must have recognized the flag stitched onto my backpack.

"No, thank you."

"Special price for you, Canada. Forty rupees." The boy was barefoot but had tiny gold earrings the size of poppy seeds. "Boys or girls can wear. Buy one for your girlfriend."

"I don't have a girlfriend."

"You know why you don't have a girlfriend? Because you don't have a bracelet!" The boy smiled with mischievous eyes.

He reminded me of my neighbourhood friends—we were enterprising kids once, too, shovelling driveways after every snowfall for five dollars. We'd bring Ally and the younger kids, who carried mini-shovels with cartoon characters printed on them. Once the customers agreed and shut their doors, we'd signal a couple of the older kids to join us and do most of the actual shovelling.

"Can't argue with that," I said, and pulled a few small bills from my pocket, not bothering to bargain down the price this time.

I pointed to a yellow-and-white bracelet, and the boy said, "That's a very good one. Will always keep you on the right path." He flipped the cardboard over, released a knot, then tied the bracelet around my wrist with small hands that looked much older than they were.

The boy said thank you and ran off, and I went back to looking up and down the road for my uncle. Scanning the faces that passed, I worried I wouldn't be able to recognize him. Why hadn't I asked him on the phone what he was wearing? I had only met my uncle as a young child and remembered little of that trip with my parents. I hoped I'd be able to identify him from photos, and my mom's stories. "Quinton's as tall as sugar cane. He's gone thin with age, but he's still got his strength. He has to, to live in that house alone."

My eyes darted from face to face. I checked my phone—no calls, the battery dying. I didn't want to risk calling and have to go searching for a place to plug in. I hoped Uncle didn't go to the bar looking for me.

And then there he was, a familiar face making his way through a crowd of market shoppers. Uncle Quinton wore a faded cotton dress shirt and khaki slacks. His worried expression I would see often in the coming days.

I waved my arm and called out, "Uncle!"

"Aiden, you made it!" He came over and pulled me in for a hug, but my backpack prevented him from getting his arms around me. "How was the journey?"

"Good. I didn't get much sleep on the bus, but when the sun came up I enjoyed seeing all the green hills and villages. I'm ready to explore Goa now."

"There'll be time for that. You must be tired. Come, we'll go home." He led me to a line of scooters just off the road. They all looked identical, but he stopped at one, turned the key to lift up the seat, and pulled out a helmet. He put the helmet on, closed the seat, and sat down.

"You only have one helmet?" I asked.

"By law only the driver needs a helmet. Come, sit."

That didn't make me feel at ease, but with my backpack on, I awkwardly straddled the scooter and sat down behind him.

Uncle Quinton started the engine and manoeuvred us toward the main road. I wasn't sure what I was supposed to hold on to and thought I should ask before I just looped my arms around his chest. But I didn't get the chance. My uncle pulled onto the road and hit the gas, and the weight of my backpack pulled me backwards. I tried to grab the back of his shirt but it slipped from my grasp and I fell off the scooter, landing on my left arm. Vehicles swerving around me madly honked their horns, but I didn't move until I felt a hand helping me up and off the road.

"You okay, Canada?" The boy with the bracelets loomed over me.

"Yes, thank you." But I felt a pain in my arm and held it up—next to my bracelet a pink scrape began to bleed. "I thought this thing was supposed to keep me on the right path."

"Right path can be bumpy," the boy said, with a subtle wobble of this head.

My uncle had circled back. "Aiden, are you okay?"

"Yes, I'm fine. Just a small cut."

"Arrey, you have to hold on at the back. I think that backpack is too big." He helped me take my pack off, laid it on the scooter floor, and rested his legs on top. He took a bill out of his front shirt pocket and slipped it to the boy. When I got back on, I held the metal bar behind the seat as tight as I could, and we were off once again.

"Molly! Enough!" Uncle shouted.

The dog had amber fur and a lean build; she was running and barking on the other side of a waist-high stone wall that surrounded his house. The weathered stone had a diamond pattern chiselled into it.

I let Molly sniff my hand through the gate while Uncle parked the scooter beside the house. Some of the orange clay tiles on the roof were darkened or discoloured, and sheets of corrugated metal slanted down over the two front windows, like eyelashes over dark eyes.

"This is the house my mother grew up in?"

Uncle nodded, and I felt a strong connection to the place, like I was staring at my own personal museum. I wanted to know everything.

Uncle led me through the gate and unlocked the front door with a key. Molly brushed past my leg and raced in.

Stepping inside felt like going down into a basement on a hot summer day. The front room had a small television in one corner, a radio with cassette tapes piled on top, two chairs in the centre, and an altar on the wall with framed pictures of Jesus and Mary, crosses, candles, and crucifixes. Molly ran around sniffing my pants and bag, before lying down by the chairs.

Uncle placed the palm of his hand flat against the wall, which was the same colour as the outside of the house: light yellow, like the inside of a banana. "Blocks of iron ore stone, covered with limestone plaster. Over a century old."

I touched the wall, too—cool and chalky. I tried to imagine how such massive stone blocks were moved back then, and pictured the houses in *The Flintstones.*

"And the floor." He stomped his sandal on the hard, smooth surface. "Cow dung."

I stared at the brown, cement-like floor and sniffed the air for a scent I had failed to detect.

My cell phone vibrated in my pocket.

"Hi, Aiden, Maria speaking. Did you reach?" My cousin's slow and soft voice was comforting to hear again.

"Yes, thank you, Maria. I literally just walked in the door." I was worried my phone would die and dug for my charger in my backpack.

"Good, I prayed you'd be safe on your journey."

I held up the charger to Uncle, and he directed me to an outlet. "How did your prayer meeting go?" I asked Maria, but when Uncle Quinton's face turn to disappointment, I regretted asking this in front of him.

"Oh, it was good. I won't talk long, just wanted to see you made it. And I forgot to ask what time you'll be coming back on the twenty-fourth?"

"One sec, let me get my ticket from my bag. Do you want to talk to your dad?"

There was a slight hesitation before she said, "Okay."

I handed the phone to her father and looked for my journal, which had the ticket inside.

"Hi, Maria... I'm good. Yes, he recognized me. But you know, he happened upon an accident. Fell right off the scooter and cut his arm... Yes, I'll put ghaneddem on it."

Being reminded of the cut on my arm made it sting as I unzipped one of the side pockets of my bag and found my journal, as well as the novel I was reading, *Hullabaloo in the Guava Orchard*. A pouch in the back of the journal held my train ticket along with pictures from home. I handed the ticket to Uncle, pointing to the time.

"Arrives at VT Station at 10 p.m.," Uncle said. I couldn't hear what Maria said to him next, but he glanced at the altar, then said, "Okay then, take care. Tell your mother I will call her later. Okay, bye."

I felt guilty then that I'd be leaving Uncle Quinton alone here for Christmas, and I'd be in Mumbai with Maria, her mother, and Aunt Delilah.

Uncle handed back the phone but held on to the ticket.

"Seven hundred rupees you paid? Upper class. When I go to Mumbai, it costs me forty rupees."

"The regular-class seats were all booked."

He passed the ticket back with a humph, and I couldn't help feeling like he thought I was spoiled.

"Come, let's take care of that cut." He led me down the hallway, past a room with two single beds, past the kitchen to the right, and out the door to the backyard.

Ten feet away was an outhouse with the same walls and roof as the house. Maria had warned me when I was in Mumbai that there was only an outhouse here: "Dad put a door on it a while back. Before that, you had to sing when you were using the toilet, so no one would come in. And when I was young, some people had a piggy toilet. The waste would go down and be cleared by the pigs. The gross thing was that some people would then eat those same pigs."

"Be careful of the well." Uncle pointed to an open hole below the kitchen window about half the size of the outhouse. "It's a lot of effort to get someone out." The well had a pulley and rope with a copper pot tied to one end to fetch the water through the window. I peeked over the edge at the water far below and took a step back. Why hadn't he put a railing around the hole?

Molly followed us outside, trotted past the well, and lay down in a spot in the shade.

Uncle's eyes were on the ground as he casually walked around the well, past the outhouse and toward one of the stone walls separating his backyard from the neighbours'. These walls were made from round rocks stacked one on top of the other and enclosed a few towering trees in the yard before being taken over by jungle farther back.

"Is that a mango tree?" I recognized the leaves from a small potted one my mom grew back home.

"Yes, but it's not the season. In summer that tree is full of mangoes. Hundreds." His eyes remained on the ground, like he was looking for a four-leaf clover.

"Do you eat them?"

"Of course. The neighbours come also. We pick some early, but by the time they get ripe we're eating mangoes for breakfast, lunch, and dinner."

Uncle stopped, bent down, and tore off the leaves of what looked like a weed.

"Come," he said, placing the leaves on the stone wall.

As I approached, I heard a voice from the other side of the wall. "Uncle, have you seen my cock-a-doodle-do? I can't find him." The speaker was a little girl in a ponytail and pink T-shirt.

"No, I haven't seen that rooster of yours," Uncle said. "Probably out gallivanting."

"He's a naughty fellow," she said, then pointed at me. "Who's that?"

"Priscilla, this is Aiden. Clara Auntie's son, from Canada."

"Where's that?"

"Very far away. By plane you have to go."

Priscilla smiled; her two front teeth were missing. There was a world map in my journal I wanted to show her, but she was pointing to the leaves Uncle had picked. "You got hurt?"

"Not too bad."

"He fell right off the back of the scooter," Uncle said.

Priscilla stared at me like she'd never heard of anyone doing such a thing.

"I've never ridden on a scooter before. I didn't know you were supposed to hold on at the back." I turned to Uncle. "You're not going to tell everyone, are you?"

But he just held the plant ready, indicating that I was to rest my arm on the wall. He rubbed the leaves above it like he was handwashing a piece of clothing. A strong, unpleasant smell filled the air, and liquid from the leaves dripped into the cut.

"Ow!" I hadn't expected it to sting.

"Hurts, yes. But it's a very good antiseptic. This will clear it."

Later, I thought, I would dress the wound properly with the first-aid pack I had in my bag.

"Can I have your bracelet?" Priscilla asked.

I was going to give it to her, but Uncle answered before I could. "Priscilla. Hush. You don't ask like that. Now, where's your brother?"

"Pedro's playing football."

"Soccer?" I was intrigued. "Where does he play?"

"Near the church."

"Later in the day you can go," Uncle said. "Have breakfast and take rest first. Come, I still have to show you the toilet."

We said goodbye to Priscilla, who went back to searching for her rooster, and Uncle led me back to the outhouse. The door was thin and didn't have a lock. Inside, pieces of wood and tools were tucked against one wall, and around a short corner was a squatter toilet and a pail of water with a small plastic container floating inside. I had encountered the squatter toilet in Mumbai, and my leg muscles struggled to sustain the required position.

Light snuck in through the space between the walls and the roof, and a bare bulb hung from the ceiling. "Where's the switch?" I asked.

"Ah, come," Uncle said with a half smile, and led me back inside the house.

In the backroom was a red light bulb and switch, sitting above a small fridge the size of the one I had had in my dorm room. Uncle flicked the switch and the red light went on.

"I put this in a while ago to turn the outside light on, too. So just flick this switch before and after you go."

"It's a smart idea. What was it like here when my mom was growing up, with so many people in this house?"

"Chaos."

He didn't elaborate further, and I wished Maria had come here with me—all of her stories were about people. When I'd asked her when the last time she'd come to Goa was, she went quiet, then answered, "It's been a long time." When I asked her if she didn't like it there, she said, "I love it, but Brother Abraham says we must let go of what we love." I didn't agree with this but couldn't find a way to tell her that wouldn't contradict her beliefs.

Uncle flicked the switch off and said, "This bulb will probably go soon, though; I haven't changed it yet."

"I heard they're working on light bulbs that could last up to twenty-five years." This was one of the few things I'd retained from my chemistry professor's lectures.

"I don't think I like the idea of a light bulb lasting longer than I will," Uncle said, moving into the kitchen. "Sit, I'll make some tea."

I sat on the grainy wood chair and rested my arms on a matching table. Looking around, I wondered how many meals my mother had had in this kitchen.

Jolting upright in bed, I woke to the sound of something shattering. The tangle and blur of the white mosquito net confused me as I struggled to get out from under it. It was still daytime, and light came in through the windows. Uncle's bed was empty. I went to the front door, where Molly was barking. The almost thunderous cracking from above went in waves, then stopped.

A boy was peeking in through the window. "Monkeys," he said.

Uncle came rushing in from the back of the house. "Are they still out there?"

"It's okay, Uncle, I chased them away with stones."

"Good job, Pedro."

"Monkeys?" I asked, taking a step back from the window.

"In between the trees they run on roofs, and sometimes knock down the tiles," the boy said. "It doesn't happen too often, so you should feel lucky—not everyone gets the monkeys welcoming them."

Monkeys!

"But they know what they're doing," Uncle said. "They wait for midday, when people are napping."

Pedro hoisted himself up on the window ledge. "Priscilla said you play football?"

"Yes," I said. So this was Priscilla's brother.

"You should come play."

"Let him eat first. I'll take him to the tea stall and then I'll drop him off at the field after."

Pedro agreed, and dropped down from the window.

Uncle and I locked up the house and took a two-minute scooter ride to a tiny tea stall tucked in between several banana trees. Dark metal tables and chairs were arranged under the shade of a roof of thatched coconut leaves. A glass display held candies and sweets, and bottles of cashew fenny were lined up on a shelf behind the counter.

As soon as we sat down, a man came and poured us water in steel cups. Uncle said something in Konkani to him, and he took away my cup of water. He returned a moment later with a bottle of water and two steaming cups of chai.

"Your mother told me you left school," Uncle said, picking up his cup and blowing steam away from the rim.

"I can go back if I want," I said quickly, and tried to take a sip of my chai, but it was far too hot. I thought back to that year of engineering. It had been a shock at first to have so many other Indian students in my class, coming from a town where my sister and I were the only ones. In my engineering circle, my nickname was Coconut—brown on the outside, white on the inside. I didn't like that name: it implied I was missing something, or faking or concealing my identity. But as the semester wore on, that began to feel true.

248

"I'm glad you can go back. But you should have finished your studies first, then come."

"But I needed to come now." I put the tea down. "I did well in my courses first semester, but things changed second semester when I went to the bookstore to buy my textbooks. On the way to the checkout, I stopped at a table and picked up a copy of Rohinton Mistry's *A Fine Balance*. I didn't read a word of my textbooks until I finished that book. Soon after, I felt India calling me."

The waiter returned with two plates filled with potato and onion bhajias.

"India will be here. And I will show you Goa. But your education is very important." Uncle picked up a bhajia and took a small bite. He blew steam from the fried treat before popping it into his mouth.

"Did you go to school, Uncle?"

"Of course. I went to VJTI, a technical institute in Bombay. I got my Weaving Manufacturing Certificate. Then I was able to get a job for Swadeshi Mills, part of Tata."

"What did you do, though?"

"Textiles. We took cotton and made cloth. Nowadays everything is electronic, but back then we used huge looms. 'Swinging monsters,' we used to call them. It started with Platt Brothers looms, plain looms. Then came the Japanese Sakamoto looms; these were semi-automatic. And by the time the shuttleless Nuovo Pignone looms came out, I was Assistant Weaving Master." He described each loom like it was an old friend.

"How long were you there?"

"Twenty-five years. But the price of land in Bombay went through the roof, so they moved the whole operation to Gujarat. Everyone lost their job. I was almost fifty, and no one hired you that old. We fought for years to get the pension we were owed. In the end we got half of what we were supposed to. Although, without it, I don't know what I'd do."

I felt guilty for having worked just a few months after leaving school and being able to afford the plane ticket to travel here. Just as I thought about leaving some money for him when I left, the waiter brought the bill. I reached for my wallet, but Uncle pulled the bill away and paid it.

"It would be different if Maria was working or married, but she isn't. I'm still supporting her." Uncle downed the last of his chai as if it were a shot of alcohol.

"Kitem adlem nisteak?" one of the boys playing soccer asked me.

I shook my head. "I'm sorry. I only speak English, unfortunately."

Pedro replied to the boy, then said to me, "He's asking what you got for fish today."

"Fish?"

"What food you ate? Your meal. We eat fish for lunch so often, everyone just asks what kind."

"Oh. I didn't have fish, but my meal was very tasty."

The seven other boys were all different ages and all barefoot. After Uncle had dropped me off, I wasn't so sure about playing. The field had a slight slant, then dropped off precipitously on one side. The earth was hard: red dirt, with tiny, rounded stones scattered everywhere that the boys called "xencare."

We divided into teams and began to play; the kids were half my age but all fast and strong on the ball. Pedro was on the opposite team and the best of the bunch—I couldn't get the ball off him. Running on the small stones was difficult at first, and I slipped around a bit.

After Pedro scored his fourth goal in the metal nets with no mesh, I asked him, "Will you play for Portugal or India?"

"Football I'd play for Portugal. Cricket I'd play for India."

There was once a time I'd dreamed of playing soccer for Canada.

It felt great to do something I did back home and was good at, but after half an hour, I hadn't got off a single decent shot. The game was out of reach, but I still wanted to score at least one goal to prove myself. Maybe it was because I was older and not born here, but I wanted to show them a Goan from Canada could really play, too. I was near the edge of the field and kicked the ball with the outside of my foot. The ball sailed toward the net, but I lost track of it when I skidded on the small stones—I landed on my side and slid down the hill. I could feel my right arm scraping the ground before my slide turned into a roll.

When I opened my eyes, Pedro was running down the hill.

"Are you alright?" he asked when he reached me.

"I think so," I said, embarrassed. Then I remembered about the shot. "Did I score?"

Pedro looked like he wanted to lie, but then he shook his head.

"Damn," I said.

"It was close," Pedro added. The church bells rang, and he said, "Time to go home."

We said goodbye to the other kids, and Pedro and I walked back together. Seeing the scrape on my arm, he said, "Come, I know a plant for that."

"No thank you," I said, remembering the sting of the last one.

"This won't hurt, it's just aloe."

We stopped off at Pedro's house and he broke a leaf off the spiked aloe plant growing in his front yard. He told me to hold out my arm and with two fingers squeezed the gel from the leaf. I spread it over the scrape and felt a cooling sensation. I didn't notice my uncle Quinton walk up behind us.

"What happened?" he asked. Molly followed close behind, tongue out and tail wagging.

"I'm fine. Just slipped down the hill while playing."

"What will your mother say?"

I felt like a child again. I repeated, "I'm fine."

"You have to be careful."

"Uncle, you didn't give him fish for lunch?" Pedro asked.

"No. Tomorrow we'll have to get one. Aiden, after church I'll show you the beaches and we'll get a fresh fish."

The mass was in Konkani, so I understood none of it, but was surprised by how similar many of the actions and the order of events were to services at home. After the mass, everyone mingled outside, near the large white statue of St. Francis of Assisi. When I saw the cemetery and path leading up a large hill, I recalled distant memories of a story I'd been told by my father. Something involving coconuts rolling down the hill and a bad priest. I remembered he'd said he would tell me the full story when I was older.

Before I could ask Uncle about it, Priscilla and Pedro came rushing toward us. She was in a dress, and he wore dress pants and a shirt. They switched from trying to be the first to tell me something to saying back and forth, "You tell him!" "No, you tell him," and laughing too hard for me to understand.

Finally, Priscilla calmed enough to invite me and Uncle to dinner tomorrow.

I looked to Uncle, who nodded.

"That sounds great, Priscilla. Thank you," I said. "Did you find your rooster?"

"No, he's still missing."

"Probably got eaten by a snake," Pedro joked.

"I'm sure he'll turn up," Uncle said.

"Can you play football today?" Pedro asked.

"We're going to see the beaches today," Uncle said.

As we said goodbye to the pair, I felt a small acceptance at their invitation to dinner and to play soccer again, even after hurting myself.

We went back to Uncle's scooter and, after making a stop to change out of our church clothes at his house, we began the journey. I held on to the back of the scooter this time. We went to three beaches that day, each with a different seductive meeting of sand and sea. The first beach was mostly filled with pale Europeans lying on cabana chairs under large umbrellas and being served drinks. The next beach had only Indian tourists. They took pictures and frolicked in the shallow water in their ordinary clothes instead of swimwear; this made me smile, remembering how my aunt Delilah did the same on a trip to Sauble Beach long ago. I would have to remind her when I returned to Mumbai.

As we approached the third beach on Uncle's scooter, we passed what looked like a slum. The small houses were a patchwork of corrugated metal, plastic, and thatched coconut leaves. Clothes hung on short lines. Women in saris washed pots near a well. A few kids were flying kites, while others laughed as they rolled an old tire back and forth.

We parked the scooter and walked down to the beach. This one felt more authentic than the others. Maybe because there were fewer people, and all of them locals. But there was something else as well. Something about the water and trees that felt familiar—the scene reminded me of a picture that hung in the living room of my parents' house and had been in my dreams since I was young. Sitting in the sand and watching the water, I felt like I'd stepped back into one of those dreams.

As we returned to the scooter, Uncle stopped at a table that held a stack of coconuts. The leaves in the tall trees behind them moved in the breeze like shaggy hair atop a head.

There were two men at the stand; the younger one carried a machete.

"Two," Uncle said in English. "One tender coconut for my nephew."

"Very good." The merchant made a kind of checkmark in the air with his head. He spoke in Konkani to the young man, who sliced the tops off two coconuts. He handed one to my uncle and another to me; a plastic straw floated in the water filled almost to the brim.

The merchant turned to me as I drank and asked, "Where are you from, my friend?"

"Canada. How did you know I'm not from here?" I hadn't spoken yet and wasn't wearing my backpack.

The coconut seller chuckled. "You have hope in your eyes. Too much hope for here."

The water I was drinking went down the wrong pipe and I started coughing. I cleared my throat and said I was okay, before coughing again and turning toward the beach.

"Too much hope," Uncle said. "Guess how much he paid for a train ticket to Mumbai?"

The merchant leaned in.

"Seven hundred."

"Aye-ye-ye-ya," the man said, then translated to the young man. Both of them looked at me like they were simultaneously impressed that I had spent that much and that I was foolish for doing so.

"They were sold out," I repeated, clearing my throat again.

But Uncle had finished his drink and was paying the man fifteen rupees.

"Did this one cost more?" I asked the merchant.

"Yes, that's a tender coconut. The young ones cost more."

"Why?" I asked.

"The older ones we can just drop to the ground," the coconut seller said. "But the young ones would get bruised or broken, so we have to lower them down with a rope. Takes more time."

I took a slow sip and looked up at the coconut tree behind him. "I used to dream of climbing coconut trees when I was younger."

"So long as you don't dream *under* the coconut tree." The man let out another chuckle. "Might be your last if one falls and hits your head."

"You used to climb them, right?" I asked Uncle. "I remember hearing stories of you spending whole afternoons up the coconut trees."

"That was a long time ago." Uncle looked at the other merchant stalls down the road, squinting in the sun. "Let me see if I can go get one fish. You'll stay here?"

Uncle left, I finished the water, and the young man split the coconut and gave me a small piece of shell to scrape the tender flesh from the inside.

The merchant must have noticed me staring at the trees. "You want to climb?"

"I probably shouldn't."

"Come. It's not too difficult."

I thought of Uncle coming back and finding me up in a coconut tree. I wanted to show him that I could indeed do it.

The merchant spoke in Konkani to the young man with the machete, who moved to the closest tree behind him and waved me over. I joined him at the tree, and he put both hands around the trunk and made a pulling motion. Then he angled his feet so they almost curled around the trunk. One hand after the other, he moved higher, shimmying his feet up in stride.

My sister, Ally, and I had climbed many trees back in Canada, but none without branches. I put my arms around the tree, like

255

the young man had. The trunk had ringed ridges and the bark was as coarse as sandpaper. Though my feet didn't bend the way the young man's did, I pulled with my arms and pushed with my feet as hard as I could, moving my body upward.

"That's it! You're a natural," the merchant shouted from below.

Up among the fronds, the young man was hanging on with one arm and smiling, encouraging me on. I imagined myself at the top, calling down to my uncle in triumph. A great story to tell when I got back home.

But I soon began to feel the strain in my arms and legs, and my climbing slowed. When my muscles started shaking, I stopped, wrapping my arms and legs around the tree and hugging it as tight as I could.

I looked up. The young man was waiting for me.

"Take a break, it's okay," the merchant shouted from below.

I glanced down at him. "I think that's as far as I can go."

"You're sure?"

"Yes. How do I get down?"

"Slide, slowly."

I loosened my grip but didn't move. I could feel sweat on my forehead and I wanted to wipe it away but couldn't. When I loosened my grip more, I descended too rapidly. The inside of my thighs and chest chafed against the tree trunk as I tried to regain my hold. When I finally stopped sliding, I hugged the tree even tighter than I had before.

The young man climbed down the other side of the tree to the ground. He stood below me, and I felt his hands around my waist. I loosened my grip, and he helped lift me to the ground.

I was relieved when I felt the sand and stone beneath me. I stayed sitting there for a few seconds, but my back straightened when I heard my uncle's voice.

"Aiden, what are you doing?" He was carrying a plastic bag with the fish inside.

"I just thought I'd try."

"You're not from here. You could have gotten really hurt. What would I have done then?"

I sat there with fresh scrapes stinging my legs and chest and my uncle standing over me. I glanced up at the top of the tree again, but it seemed impossibly high and out of reach.

When I stood up and brushed myself off, Uncle added to the humiliation, saying, "Tomorrow I'm not going to let you out of my sight."

The next afternoon, Uncle and I sat in the tea stall again, drinking chai and eating Parle-G biscuits.

"What time is your train tomorrow morning?" he asked, speaking louder than usual as a crow was cawing in the surrounding trees.

"Ten-thirty." I dunked a biscuit into my tea, but when I pulled it out, the wet half crumbled into the cup. I pulled my chair in closer to the table and felt the bite of the cuts and scrapes all over my body.

"You'll arrive on Christmas Eve. Maria will be happy." Uncle dipped his biscuit in his tea twice, for only a second or two so it didn't fall apart. "Just make sure she doesn't take you to that cult. Or has she already?"

The cawing crow was joined by others, and I had to almost shout. "She took me, but don't worry, there's no chance of me joining."

The racket in the trees grew louder until it reached an uproar. As we waited for the commotion to subside, I thought back to that evening in Mumbai with Maria. From outside, the building where the prayer services were held had looked like a government office. The inside was simple as well, with pews, an altar, and a hall where everyone sat on the floor after the service. Maria introduced me to Brother Abraham. He was a short man, about five foot two, with a thick moustache and all the charisma and confidence of a leader. When we were walking home later, Maria asked me what I thought of him.

"He's very...passionate," I said, trying not to offend her.

There was a lone, dim street light on the road we walked on, but otherwise it was only lit from the light leftover from the houses. "You walk this way alone, Maria?"

"Yes. I like to look into the houses as I pass them, and see how people live," she said. "What did you think of the service?"

"I don't think I'll ever join any religion myself, but I'm glad you've found something that interests you."

"That's okay. You know my father doesn't approve of me going. But he doesn't understand how much it means to me. I'm going to be part of this my whole life," she said with certainty.

The crows quieted, and the customers' chatter resumed. Uncle finished his cup of chai and said, "You know, when your father came, he brought me one bottle of Johnny Walker. I hardly ever drink, only one glass on holidays, but Maria poured the whole bottle down the drain because Brother Abraham says drinking is evil. If I ever meet that fellow I'd have many words for him."

I felt the urge to defend Maria then. "I met him when I went. He's not someone I'd ever consider following, but I didn't think he was a horrible person. I can see how it would be frustrating, though, if he's telling people to pour liquor down the drain."

"You know that group doesn't follow the Church's teachings. I should have forbidden Maria from going. I had no idea they would take my daughter away."

"I'm sorry," I said, and wanted Maria to hear how he felt.

"Our priest recently warned us about this group. He said it

was dangerous. If only they'd told us about it back when Maria joined."

The crow let out a single caw. I paused for a second to see if it would continue, but we were spared.

"She seems happy," I said. "And I don't think it's dangerous. They seemed like nice people, and what they do isn't that much different from the Catholic Church. Actually, the most dangerous part, I thought, was walking back from their meeting hall at night."

"I've tried telling her how many times not to walk at night. Her mother always used to say she has no fear. Even as a little girl she wasn't afraid of anything. I remember there was one day, when she was eight or nine years old, and I heard her talking to someone in the backyard. I looked out the kitchen window and saw a cobra standing right next to her."

"A king cobra?"

"Yes." Uncle motioned to the waiter, who refilled his cup. He blew gently along the surface of his chai and took a sip before continuing. "So I rushed outside. My first instinct was to pull her away, but the snake was too close. If I made a sudden move, it might strike." Uncle's leg now started to move up and down, his heel tapping the ground. "It was a horrible feeling, not being able to protect her."

"What happened next?"

"I heard Maria's voice again. She spoke to the snake like it was a person: 'Why are you here? This isn't a place for you. You need to go back home.' And then, as if the snake understood, it lowered itself to the ground and slithered out of the backyard, into the jungle."

Maria hadn't told me this story, but I could so easily picture her saying these things. When we were in Mumbai, the first thing I noticed about her was how she spoke, as if each word were selected with special care. However, what I soon came to

259

appreciate most in Maria was how serene she was. I wondered if her tranquility came from knowing precisely who she was, where she came from, and why she was here.

Uncle and I sat in silence for a few minutes, listening to the chatter around us. "I remember when she was young," he continued, "everyone thought Maria was older than she was. The other kids would always come to her when they needed advice and didn't want to ask an adult. Even the adults spoke to her as if she were grown-up."

"You know what," I said. "That evening I went with Maria, after the service, the followers gathered around Brother Abraham to chat and ask his advice. But there were more people lined up to see Maria and get *her* advice. She's still helping others find their way."

For a moment there was a proud grin in the corner of Uncle's mouth, but he caught himself and said, "She's always been good with people."

The meal at Priscilla and Pedro's was simple and delicious. Rice, chapatti, and two curries were served. One clam, one fish, both so succulent and rich in flavour I was tempted to lick my plate after a second helping. Their house was similar to Uncle's, and the children gave me a tour. I felt ashamed when I asked Pedro, "Where's your room?"—I'd forgotten that most families here slept in the same room.

Outside, they showed me the small manger they'd made by hand, and told me about the contest in the village for the best one. Back inside, we sat down on their couch and I finally showed Priscilla where Canada was on the map at the back of my journal. She saw the pictures in the pocket and pulled them out.

Priscilla and Pedro asked who was who in each picture, but

the one they were most fascinated by was one of my favourites, too. It was a picture Ally had taken when we were kids, in the field near our home. It was of two snow-covered evergreens in the distance and a young sapling up close with snow falling all around.

"What's snow like?" Pedro asked.

Before I could think of how to describe it, Priscilla asked, "Does it burn you when falling?"

"No, it just melts."

"It's so pretty," she said.

"Everyone back home would say *this* place is pretty." I felt sad then, knowing I'd be leaving Goa tomorrow. "One day you'll both have to come visit."

They kept staring at the picture. They had far too much wonder in their eyes for me not to give it to them so they could imagine a world they had never seen before. I had done the same with Goa. I thought then how much more precious the dreams of the young were—they could so easily be crushed or broken.

The next morning, Uncle and I ate a quick breakfast of tea and toast. I had packed my bag the previous night but did a final check to make sure I didn't forget anything. Molly had been trailing me the whole morning and began to lick my heels.

"She knows you're leaving," Uncle said, and asked if I had packed everything.

I zipped up my backpack and said yes, and told him I just had to go to the washroom. He said he'd go fill gas in the scooter and went out the front door.

I flicked the light on for the outhouse. So Molly couldn't escape, I opened the back door just enough to slide my body out. I entered the outhouse and closed the door behind me.

The door slammed harder than I had intended, and I thought I heard movement in the pile of wood, but figured the door closing had just dislodged it.

As I pulled my pants back up, I heard a much louder noise come from the wood, like onion tossed into a pan of hot oil. Disbelieving, I saw a snake's head float out from the wood. Its body followed, dark brown and shiny. Two metres of it slithered along the ground, looping and coiling to block the door.

Molly began to bark fiercely from inside the house. My instincts arrived a few moments later. I grabbed a stick from the pile and held it like a baseball bat, ready.

The cobra spread its hood and rose to half my height.

I took a half step back, but there was nowhere for me to go.

The snake hissed again. Looking into its eyes was both mesmerizing and terrifying. The cobra flicked its tongue and moved its head in a wide circle.

It was then, in the middle of my panic, that a strange and calming thought came to me. The way the snake bobbed its head was just like the way so many people here did.

"Easy," I said, lowering the stick very slowly. "I'm not going to hurt you."

The snake remained standing.

I took two long, deep breaths. Gently, I said, "You need to go home."

The snake stood for a few seconds more, then lowered to the ground. It flicked its tongue twice more before it turned and slithered under the door. I waited a little while in the outhouse. I wiped the sweat from my forehead. I should have been trembling, but the calm feeling that had come over me remained. Once Molly stopped barking, I opened the door.

The train station felt relaxed compared to the ones in Mumbai, and the peace I'd felt after the snake stayed with me. Uncle and I sat drinking chai, waiting for my train. I put the three postcards I'd bought at the station into my journal: one each for Ally, Eric, and my parents.

"You sure you didn't find anything?" I asked.

"I checked the whole yard and Pedro and Priscilla's yard as well. Nothing. It must have gone away." He asked if I was done my chai and took my empty paper cup and put it in his. "You were very lucky. A snake in that close an area is usually deadly. You did well to stay calm."

"Thank you, Uncle," I said. "But if you hadn't told me that story with Maria, I don't think I would have survived."

Uncle looked off into the direction my train was to come from, then turned to me and said, "I think you'll have a lot of tales to tell about your time here. But look, there's your train." He pointed in the distance. "One minute, stay here. I'll be back." He rushed back to the stall where we'd bought the chai and postcards.

As the train rolled to a stop, Uncle returned, clutching a package of cashews.

"Can you give these to Maria?"

"Of course."

"They're her favourite."

I wasn't sure how I could explain to Maria the love I saw in his face at that moment.

"Take care, Aiden."

"You too, Uncle. And thank you—for everything."

We hugged, and I wondered if I'd ever see him again.

On the train, I found my seat and put my bag away. But I held my journal tight, excited to tell my tales.

Outside the train, Uncle came up to my window and reached through the bars to shake my hand one final time.

Then the whistle blew. The train began to move.

And still Uncle walked alongside the train, holding my hand.

As the train collected speed, he jogged. He let go when it got too fast, but kept running beside the train—and I felt it then. Whatever I'd come here to find. What I thought I'd been missing. Running alongside me.

Acknowledgements:

I am incredibly grateful that this book has made it into the world, and into your hands. I did not always think this would be the case. *Coconut Dreams* is in some ways the book I would have loved to have read growing up, but it never made its way to me. I strongly believe that seeing oneself in stories is important—for everyone.

I would like to thank:

Jay and Hazel for believing in this book and in me, striving to make the literary world more inclusive, and bringing so much warmth and authenticity to all you do. Stuart—thank you for your love of language and such thorough work. Malcolm—thank you for your understanding, and all of your efforts on this wonderfully designed book. Pasha—thank you for diving into this complicated project and providing such shrewd and insightful suggestions. I have learned so much by seeing how you think about stories.

Early readers, writing groups, and supporters over the years for your feedback and community. Thank you, Sabrina Ramanan, Ron Schafrick, Deepa Shankaran, Adam Elliott Segal, Becky Blake, Mia Herrera, Sanjay Talreja, Rebecca Fisseha, Terese Pierre, Kathy Friedman, Tina Surdivall, Jane Foo, Sharon Overend, Robin Sutherland, Simone Dalton, Phillip Morgan, Darren Bradley Jones, Djamila Ibrahim, Julia Chan, Sonya Wilson, Emily Stilwell, Matthew Ogden, Joelle Moutou, and many others.

The University of Toronto School of Continuing Studies. Most of these stories were initially workshopped there. The feedback and words of encouragement from classmates and instructors kept me going. Thank you, Lee Gowan and everyone at the school, for being so supportive over the years. Kim Echlin—your guidance during the final project and unrelenting belief in my writing made all the difference. My heartfelt appreciation to Alissa York and Kathryn Kuitenbrouwer for your support, along with Denis Bock, Kelli Deeth, Kent Nussey, Catherine Graham, Ibi Kaslik, and Michael Winter. You have all taught me so much, and I still sometimes hear your voices when I am writing and editing.

The literary journals and editors that published earlier versions of these stories. Thank you, *The Rusty Toque, Joyland, Cosmonauts Avenue, The Writers' Community of Durham Region, Maple Tree Literary Supplement, The Antigonish Review, Switchback Magazine, The Fieldstone Review, Shorthand* (Diaspora Dialogues), *The Dalhousie Review*, and *Three* (University of Toronto/Penguin Random House). Special thanks to Kathryn Mockler, as well as Amatoritsero Ede, Veronica Ross, Sheheryar B. Sheikh, Jennifer Lambert, Bükem Reitmayer, and Madeleine Maillet.

Helen Walsh, Zalika Reid-Benta, and everyone past and present involved in Diaspora Dialogues. The connections, support, and programs made the publishing world easier to navigate and the process less daunting. Thank you, Andrew J. Borkowski, for your amazing workshop, and Cynthia Holz, for your astute mentoring and advancement of each of these stories.

The Toronto Arts Council for your support. The Ontario Arts Council, Jack Illingworth, Bushra Junaid, Phoebe Wang, and everyone involved in Fuel for Fire. Jael Richardson and the many people that make FOLD possible. I first met Jay and Hazel at these events—having the time and space for those conversations was invaluable.

All those who organize and put on reading series and literary events, as well as helping folks feel comfortable at them. Special thanks to the Emerging Writers Reading Series, Mahak Jain, Marcia Walker, and Jess Taylor.

Matthew Whitten for generously sharing your story with me. Anosh Irani for answering my email many years ago. Lee Maracle for your feedback on "Hold It Like a Butterfly." Also, thank you to some of the women in my life and writing circles who helped shape "Snapshots"—I wouldn't have attempted it without your direction and voices.

All the families that shared our small pocket of Burlington, especially the children of Forestwood, Deerhurst, and Blue Spruce.

My many Bal Ashram brothers and sisters; please know I cherish our connection and time together.

Dear friends over the years (you know who you are) for sharing your lives with me, for being there for me, and for understanding. Thank you to the Ravens for the many memories. And thank you to all of my current and former colleagues for your encouragement and friendship.

The D'Souza, Mascarenhas, Fernandes, Rattos, Rebello, Correia, D'Costa, Pinto, Montazeri, Benoit, and Carney families, as well as all of the Hamilton picnic and Goan families.

Nunna, Pappa, Mai, Pai, Sabina, Ozzy, Nisha, Mila, Gaurav, Prashant, Zachary, Angela, Arlette, Joaquim, Julie, Rev, Vamsi, Joe, Maggie and family, Joaquim, Lorraine and family—I am very lucky to have experienced India through your guidance. While any inaccuracies remain my own, I also want to thank Florinda Da Silva for help with the Konkani words.

My great-auntie Nita for telling me ghost stories from your childhood in Goa, and so much more. Theresa D'Souza—your resounding laughter, wisdom, and heart are missed often.

Christine, Merces, Troy, Sherwin, Raul, Travis, and (baby #2) for a lifetime of loving memories. My parents—I couldn't have asked for more love and support every step of the way. Dad—I have always admired your genuineness and ability to connect with people, and I am fortunate your values and work ethic were instilled in us at a very young age. Mom—you have been my first storyteller, reader, editor, and inspiration; you will always be my hero. Ash, Miss, and Jo—I am so lucky to have shared my childhood with you and watched you become the adults you are. I appreciate all you've done over the years; so much of this book is also yours. Shan—this wouldn't have been possible without your daily support, critical thinking, and loving feedback.

I am beyond grateful.

DEREK MASCARENHAS is a graduate of the University of Toronto School of Continuing Studies Creative Writing Program, a finalist and runner-up for the Penguin Random House of Canada Student Award for Fiction, and a nominee for the Marina Nemat Award. His fiction has been published in places such as *Joyland, The Dalhousie Review, Switchback, Maple Tree Literary Supplement, Cosmonauts Avenue,* and *The Antigonish Review.* Derek is one of four children born to parents who emigrated from Goa, India, and settled in Burlington, Ontario. A backpacker who has traveled across six continents, Derek currently resides in Toronto. *Coconut Dreams* is his first book.

Colophon

Manufactured as the first edition of *Coconut Dreams*
in the spring of 2019 by Book*hug Press.

Copy edited by Stuart Ross
Type + design by Malcolm Sutton